5-Minute
Short Stories

A Bathroom Book

Michael Landolfi

5-Minute Short Stories
A Bathroom Book

This is a collection of true and invented tales. If your name appears in one of the true stories, you should be proud to have been included in this book. If your name appears in one of the fictitious yarns, it is simply a coincidence. However, you should feel complimented as I use interesting names conjured from my imagination. No offense is meant.

Written, designed and published by
Louis Michael Landolfi
Asheville, NC

ISBN-13:978-1506138923

ISBN-10:1506138926

Paperback

For

Rob Perlstein

The Bravest Man I Have Ever Met

Thanks for your encouragement.

Preface

Ask any hemorrhoid doctor – time sitting on the potty should be limited, five minutes or less is the national consensus. Nine out of 10 doctors agree that sensitive tissues at the end of the line (or on the bottom, as most folks call it) should have limited exposure to high internal pressure; too much and things can begin to swell, itch and bleed. It's uncomfortable, embarrassing, and unsightly. Yuck! Now, there's an awful thought – unsightly.

Anyway, here are 31 short stories that will help you with time management and dependent tissue care. Each can be read in 5 minutes or less, and there is one for each day of the month. Read one story, tidy up, and get off the potty. By the end of the book you will have developed a new healthy habit.

Many of the stories are recollections of true events in my life. Some are based on true events from someone else's life and some are true fiction. They are not children's bedtime stories.

No matter what the story is or isn't about, I hope you enjoy them. I hope they evoke emotion, help with your time management, and reduce your risk of needing a hemorrhoidectomy.

HAVE FUN

THANKS FOR BUYING MY BOOK

Michael Landolfi

Table of Contents

Part 1

Lucky Writer

Fiction rolls through the doorway almost daily. You wouldn't believe the things people do to assure themselves a place on the operating table. And I can't believe what we find under the sheets sometimes.

At 2am, my pager erupted – jackhammer vibrations and a fire house alarm at full volume. The text read: Code Trauma – STAT – 911!! I barely had time to put on gloves. The doors burst open. The stretcher shot through as though propelled by battlefield medics with their dying sergeant onboard. The patient's face was masked by crimson bandages. He was accompanied by ER nurses, two cops, and a teenage girl in handcuffs.

"Whatcha' got?"

"Face eating contest."

"A what?"

"Face eating contest," the nurse repeated.

The cop yanked the handcuffs hard, forcing the girl to step forward.

"Tell 'em!" he barked.

Through tears and sobs and a psychedelic fog she mumbled something.

"I can't understand you," I said.

She looked at the floor and sobbed harder. The cop said, "They were partying – beer, crystal meth. Then this guy's buddy brought out some Purple Wave to make it more interesting."

"Some what?"

"Sir, it's those bath salts. You can get it at head shops – even gas stations. It's like LSD, or something. Kids are getting real messed up with it and violent."

"OK. Oouu, that's nasty stuff."

"Yes sir, and then they started fighting and according to another witness – biting each other. But most of this happened when the friend's pit bull joined in."

"Oh my! Where's the other guy?"

The cops looked at each other and the girl wailed even louder.

"Sir, we left him back at the scene. He didn't make it."

I turned my attention to the patient. He was lying flat on the stretcher, moaning. His entire face was wrapped in blood-soaked gauze, a pool of blood under his head instead of a pillow.

"Alright, what's under the dressings?" I asked the nurse.

"A bloody mess. His face is totally mangled and he's lost a lot of blood. We had to tie him down 'cause he wouldn't let us touch him. Acting like an animal – doesn't even have an IV."

The vital sign monitor showed that his heart rate was very high, his blood pressure too low, and his oxygen level was critically low.

"Room one. Come on."

In the room, I gave the patient a shot of ketamine to put him out. Then I shoved a large bore IV in his vein while my helper gave him oxygen. After I placed a breathing tube into his lungs we started to unwrap his face. Blood poured.

"He's gonna bleed to death!" a nurse shouted.

"He's going into shock," added the doctor.

"It's lookin' bad," I said. "He might code! I'll give some epi!"

I gave the epinephrine and ripped open his shirt so we could do chest compressions or shock him if necessary.

To my surprise he had an old Superman tattoo on his chest – exactly like the ones my brother and I have and in the same place – right over his heart.

OH MY GOD! My mind reeled and I got faint. Is this my brother? The face is so torn up it's unrecognizable.

The monitors all alarmed at the same time and all of the wave forms went flat.

"Start CPR, get the code cart and shock him. I'll give more epi!" I ordered.

The nurse started pressing on the guy's chest and his arm fell out from under the sheet. I saw a ring, his wedding ring. It was just like mine.

The alarms kept screaming. They got louder and louder – impossibly loud. I slapped at the sound, silenced the alarm clock, and awakened drenched in sweat.

Snipe Hunt

"Have ya ever been fishin' on a bright sunny day? Sat on the bank and watched the little fishies play? With your hands in your pockets and your pockets in your pants, watched the little fishies do the hootchie cootchie dance?"

"No, I ain't."

"Well, ya oughta'."

"Why's that?"

"I dunno. It's just somethin' my Nanny says."

"Huh! … Well… does she know about snipes?"

"Yeah, a course!"

But I didn't.

I was almost twelve, but I'd never heard of snipes.

Me and Hugh were going to camp together that summer. I hadn't never been to a camp so, I was real excited. Hugh was my best friend. He'd gone to camp the last two summers and had a ball, but said it woulda' been better if I'd been there. He said there was a lotta snipes at that camp and maybe we could go huntin' 'em.

I asked Nanny about snipes. She laughed.

"There's no such thing as a snipe. It's a trick the older kids play on the young'uns. They're 'spossed ta only come out after dark and are real tricky. They can hear better than dogs so, you gotta be real quiet and sneak up on 'em, freeze 'em with your flashlight and chuck 'em in a bag. Everybody has to go huntin' by their selves so there ain't no extra noise. Then, the older boys sneak off and leave the little kids all alone."

"So Hugh is trying to trick me?"

"Maybe, but maybe he don't even know. Maybe some of the older boys are tricking him. My brothers went snipe huntin' and were left alone in the deep, dark forest. The older boys started howlin' like wolves and making monster noises. Pete and Tony got so scared they started to cry. Then, after a while the older boys came out of the pitch blackness and pretended to be zombies. My brothers nearly died of fright. All the kids laughed at 'em and called 'em names like yella bellies and chicken feathers Tony and pee diaper Pete."

"Huh, that ain't gonna happen to me, Nanny!"

In late spring, me and daddy was fishin' near Brevard. We drove by a sign, "Camp Greenbrier. Hey, there's the camp you and Hugh are going to. Wanna check it out?"

We parked and nosed around. It was closed until June, but we peeked in the windows and walked around the trails to the horse stables and the lake. We checked out the teepees and the canoes. It looked really neat. I asked dad if he thought there were any snipes around. He laughed and told me pretty much what Nanny had said.

Mean Bobby Green and his stupid buddy, Fat Eddie, found out that we were all going to the same camp. They were older and bigger and they started teasing me, especially at recess. I told the teacher and my parents, but it only backfired. The bullies just became more sneaky. Hugh didn't get much teasing because he was their friend already and they rode the same bus. But me and Hugh decided we would probably play some kinda' trick on 'em at camp, maybe steal their clothes when they were swimming, or put itching powder in their shorts.

A week before camp, Hugh got appendicitis and had an operation. He didn't get to go to camp. I had to go alone. Well, my big buddies, Bobby Green and Fat Eddie would be there. I hoped that maybe they'd be tired of acting like jerks and be nice to me.

I was wrong.

It was a long week. I had fun, but I missed my folks and Hugh. The bullies tormented me every chance they got. On the last day, the idea of a snipe hunt came up. We snuck out after dark, all ten of us boys. I figured Bobby and Eddie and the two older guys knew all about the trick. And I had a plan.

"The best snipe huntin' is by the lake," said the oldest boy.

Everybody fanned out. The little kids went first, they were so excited. The older boys hung back and I figured they were gonna try to scare us. When I got to the lake, I watched the flashlight beams wobbling behind me and then go out. The forest behind me was pitch black and silent except for the crickets and frogs. I turned my flashlight off. After about five minutes, I dropped a big bucket full of water in the lake. Kerplunk! Then yelled, "Help! Help! Help!" I made splashing noises, turned on my waterproof flashlight, threw it in and raced away.

"He's over there!" I heard someone holler. "I see his flashlight in the water!"

“Oh god! That stupid kid, he better not drown!” Bobby yelled as all the big kids ran onto the dock. They all dove in and started lookin’ for me, fussin’ and yelling my name. I snuck out, grabbed their shoes and tossed ‘em in the lake. They sank. I ran back into the woods. I had a second little flashlight and a pocket knife. I cut some saw briars and laid ‘em in the trail so the barefoot devils would step on ‘em. Then, I put that itchin’ powder in Bobby and Fat Eddie’s sheets. And since the girls were sleeping in the teepees that night, I snuck into their cabin, stole a bunch of underwear and put bras and panties in my buddies dirty laundry bags. Their moms would sure get a surprise when they washed those camp clothes.

Mean Bobby Green and Fat Eddie looked exhausted at breakfast and they couldn’t stop scratching.

“You boys roll in some poison ivy last night?” I asked from a safe distance. “And where’s your shoes?”

They promised to kill me and probably would have right then if the counselors hadn’t been there. I laughed in their faces, but worried about next school year. Luckily, we moved to Florida in August and I never saw Mean Bobby or Fat Eddie again.

All's Fair

We've all heard the worn out saying, "All's fair in love and war." Probably I first heard it from my grandmother. Her belief was that no matter what, her grandchildren should win the fight.

"Find a stick, a rock, a brick – whatever it takes, and beat the livin' crap outta the guy. It ain't cheatin'. You're just evenin' up the odds."

I listened to her advice and employed it a few times.

One day my best friend and I were roaming around in search of adventures. For some reason, I repeatedly berated him with another of Nanny's sayings, "If I was as stupid as you, I'd jump in a gopher hole and pull the gopher in behind me."

Well, after the 84th time McCoy knocked me down, mounted my chest, and smashed my face with his fists, I guess I deserved it. I was being an ass. Suddenly, he sprang up and sprinted off. It was as if I'd pulled a pistol and taken a shot.

A few days later, we made up and I asked why he'd run.

"I saw a big sharp rock within your reach and I know what Nanny says. I figured you'd see it in a second and kill me."

Another time I used her advice was during Marine Corps boot camp. I had been pitted against a guy from another platoon. He was issued a pugil stick and I was given apple boppers, which are basically boxing gloves. The other guy was huge. I guess the sergeants felt he needed some advantage. So, they gave him a stick in order to beat me to death.

The whistle blew, I bull-rushed him. He smacked me a couple of times as I got inside. Then, I used a judo throw and dropped him. We wrestled for a second and he took my back. I was down on all fours in a sand pit, carrying two hundred pounds of blood-thirsty savage. I grabbed one side of the stick and he looped it over my head. We struggled. My enemy's face was just behind my left ear.

"I'm gonna kill ya, ya pussy," he promised as he began to crush my trachea.

Nanny spoke in the other ear: "All's fair."

My face was in the dirt, the light bulb flashed on. I scooped a handful of sand and pitched it in the guy's eyes. He let out a scream, let go of the pugil stick, and swiped at his face with both hands. He was blinded. Instantly, I popped up, pummeled his head, snatched the stick, and whacked him three times. I won the match.

All's fair.

After Parris Island, I went to Infantry Training School. I had been meritoriously promoted to PFC and was appointed 1st squad leader. It was quite an honor and a bit abnormal for a small white guy. I was second in rank behind the guide. The guide was a big Hawaiian with an attitude. I never liked him. His job was to march at the front of the platoon on the right hand side, lead the platoon in a straight line, and carry the guidon. That's a wooden pole with a flag showing the Marine Corps emblem and company number. Each week there were competitions and only the best platoon in the company would win the privilege of carrying the flag.

I've forgotten the guide's name, so for all these years I've irreverently called him Pineapple Head. I know. It's not P.C., but that's what I've done. Anyway, one week our platoon won the guidon back from a rival platoon. Pineapple Head was so elated that he decided to push it around the squad bay like a mop, flag on the floor – an absolute no-no. The sergeant saw him. All hell broke loose. That evening we were called to a school circle, where all the privates gathered in the front of the squad bay, in a tight knot, "asshole to belly button." The lieutenant and sergeant stood rod straight, red-faced and frothing. They berated us with every curse imaginable. Pineapple Head had committed a mortal sin. We were all gonna pay. He was called to the front where our superiors cussed him, insulted his mother, and slapped his face. It's a wonder they didn't douse him with gasoline and set him on fire.

They now needed a new guide. The squad leader who could march the straightest was it. It was me.

Two days later, the word came to me that Pineapple Head was going to whip my ass 'cause I took his place. I watched my back. The next day, he followed me into the NCO's office and began a fight. Did I mention he was bigger than me? Did I mention that I don't fight fair? We exchanged blows and he knocked me onto the corporal's rack (that's a bed in civilian speak).

I glimpsed my salvation: the corporal's battle helmet was within reach. It longed to be tested. It was solid steel, bulletproof, Hawaiian kryptonite. I brained him with all my might, once, twice, and knocked him unconscious. Three, four, 'cause the helmet told me to. His limp body fell on me, trapping me on the bed. It was tough, but I rolled the big man off of me. He was out. Now, he might not remember being unconscious, but it's hard to forget broken ribs. I drilled his side with my spit-shined, steel-toed combat boots for good measure.

I strolled out of the office to fifty-some sets of eyes as big as the Hawaiian's ego and raised my arms in triumph. They gave me a hero's welcome. In a few minutes, the larger man slithered into the squad bay, defeated and demoralized. He didn't say a word and he never bothered me again.

I smiled to myself and thought I heard my grandmother say, "All's fair in love and war."

Bobbi Jean

"If ya want ta take me out, daddy's got ta get ta know ya a little bit."

"Like what, Sunday dinner or something?"

"Maybe, but he says ta come by Wednesday afternoon and ta bring your fishing pole."

Well, that was a new one. I'd met fathers before, but always at the door just before we took off.

On Wednesday about 2pm, I turned into Bobbi Jean's driveway. It led to a run-down farmhouse four miles outside of Marshall. Three dogs announced my arrival. I stayed in the Jeep until Bobbi Jean walked out on the porch and called them off.

Mr. Sawyer fussed at the dogs as he came to greet me, but then said, "Good boys. Don't you let no strangers sneak up on us. Bite 'em if ya want to."

I nervously shook his hand.

"Son, my little girl here says ya want to take her out on a date. You know she's only sixteen? She's really too young just yet, but I might let ya. Wanna know what kind'a boy ya are first."

I felt insulted. I wasn't a boy. I was seventeen and leaving for the Marine Corps in two months and told him so.

I loaded my pole and tackle into his old Ford Fairlane. As we drove, he lectured about his duties as a father and a man of faith. He warned me about taking advantage of Bobbi Jean. It was the longest 4½ miles of my life.

There were a couple of hobos at the fishing hole, drinking from the same Mason jar. Mr. Sawyer took a healthy swig and passed it to me. I pretended to take a swallow, but I only tasted it. This was too bizarre. He had just sermonized about Christian morals, the righteous path, and Jesus.

As I was faking my slug, he wiped his mouth on his sleeve and confided, "Son, the Lord never made a man feel unworthy or second rate. He took whatever He was offered. He forgave sinners, even whores."

The bums then offered cigarettes, he took two.

We didn't catch any fish and I tried to stay as far from him as reasonable. About 5pm he called to me and asked if I was hungry.

"Got this nice little place just down the road. And I'll treat."

Sadie's Roadside Café was a dump. The sanitation grade posted behind the register was 86 and the fresh trout tasted like burned toast.

"One more stop," Mr. Sawyer announced.

After driving at top speed for twenty minutes around a thousand sharp curves, we pulled into a dirt parking lot. The sign said, "The True Word of God, Disciples of Christ Pentecostal Church."

Already nauseous from the meal and the curves, I felt a new wave of sickness. Were we really going to church, now?

Yep.

"We're a little late, but it'll be awright."

He opened the door and pushed me inside. I froze after two steps. The sight and sounds sent me into a panic. The preacher held a rattlesnake high above his head. He was frantically pacing back and forth, frothing at the mouth as he shouted Bible passages.

About eighteen people were all shouting and crying and slobbering praise and thanks:

"HOLY JESUS!!"

"YES LORD, YES."

"Thank ya Jesus! Thank ya Lord!"

Some were clapping, some were crying, some held their arms high, reaching for redemption. I wanted to run, but a strong arm around my shoulders dragged me to the front.

"Praise Jesus!" daddy shouted and he clapped in rhythm with the preacher's sing-song oration. "Look son, The Lord is Almighty and He protects His children. Go on! Get closer. If yure a true believer no harm will come ta ya."

He forced me closer. A couple drops of pee escaped. And I was a true believer – I believed that snake was going to sink its teeth into my face and good ole God fearin' daddy wouldn't have to worry about me screwing his daughter.

I started to run, but Mr. Sawyer and a couple of other true believers held me fast. The preacher kept shouting and slobbering as he held out the snake in my direction. I froze. I was about to cry. The believers all reached for the snake with their free hands.

"All praise goes to You, Almighty God, all praise to Your Son, Jesus Christ," sang the preacher as he raised and lowered the serpent several times.

"Yes, Lord, yes!" replied Mr. Sawyer, who let go of me and reached out to receive the snake.

At the speed of light, the snake delivered his poison. Mr. Sawyer recoiled almost as fast. The preaching stopped momentarily, but soon resumed. The message was different now. Praises were traded for pleas: pleas for forgiveness, pleas for strength, knowledge, and understanding.

Bobbi Jean's dad's eyes popped, he held the bitten hand in his other and cried for forgiveness. Everyone watched. They wrapped his hand with a towel and ice and continued to pray as frantically as before. The victim smiled weakly as the poison circulated. In a couple of minutes he puked, and then he collapsed.

Reluctantly, he was loaded into the preacher's car and taken to the hospital. I drove the Fairlane back to his house and told Bobbi Jean what had happened. She and her mother wailed, jumped in the car and raced off. I followed in the Jeep.

At the emergency room desk, she held my hand. I kissed her tear-stained cheek and said I had to use the bathroom.

"Hurry back, hon."

I never saw Bobbi Jean again. Can ya blame me?

Mr. Sawyer survived. Like all true believers, his faith pulled him through.

The Lost Shoe

We were rambunctious. Three little chimps escaped from the zoo – apparently not possessing that critical evolutionary chromosome. We were wild.

I was nine, my brothers were seven and five. And it was a rainy day. The swimming pool was closed, but we went anyway. Rain never deterred curiosity, or creativity. Criminals love dark, wet days – fewer witnesses about and evidence washed away. We weren't criminals yet, but we'd begun our apprenticeship.

I don't know why we were allowed to run loose. "At large" is how the police described us. If our parents had been less naïve they would have fitted us with choke collars and chained us to trees before they left for work each day. Our babysitters would've been issued stun guns and handcuffs. We would've been guarded.

We were rambunctious.

This particular day, our grandmother was in charge. She patted us on our heads as we scooted out the door with promises to return if the pool didn't open soon.

These were the 60's. Simpler days. Safer? Hitler and Capone were dead and Manson still unknown. These were the days of Andy and Opie, a time when children played outside unconcerned with life's cruel realities. These were the days before school shootings and terrorist attacks – before every city had a serial killer, every neighborhood two sex offenders. We were free and unsupervised, and we took advantage of it.

The Manor pool was deserted when we arrived – not a soul to be found. And so, we explored. A few weeks earlier we'd been caught nosing around, prompting the pool manager, Mr. Lowenberg, to install pad locks everywhere. And this day everything was battened down tight. Locks were on the change rooms and the pump house, the equipment room and the super secret stairwell - rumored to lead to a tunnel that connected the Manor with the Grove Park Inn. We tried to jimmy them all with Patrick's pocket knife, but we failed.

So, with nothing better to do we took turns reaching our thin flexible arms up inside the drink machine where we could catch the edge of a soda can and yank it out. We burglarized the cigarette and cracker machines in the same manner. Now we were ready to settle down, plan our next caper, and wait for the pool to open. Of course, we had to hide out. So we squeezed into the space between the back of the machines and the stone wall. Pat and Tony lit up cigarettes, stood on a water pipe that traversed our hide out, and leaned back against the cracker machine. As they began to debate the flavor differences between Marlboros and Lucky Strikes, the machine began to tip. Apparently, it was top heavy.

During the moment between tilt and crash, time froze and we realized what was about to happen. Gravity would betray our crimes. We started to run even before the machine hit the slate patio, throwing glass and snacks everywhere.

We hauled ass. We ran like bloody chihuahuas fleeing a pack of pit bulls. We raced to the fence, hurdled over at full speed, and piled onto my bike. Tony rode on the handlebars, Patrick took the banana seat and I peddled with all my might. We sped away from the scene and escaped onto Charlotte Street.

"Faster, faster!!" screamed Patrick.

"Watch out for the telephone pole!" implored Tony from the handlebars and he began to sob.

"I'm doin' the best I can."

The load was heavy and unwieldy, my steering uncertain. I was standing, peddling, steering, and freaking out. My heart and legs were pumping at an Olympic pace. When we came to Hillside Walk, Tony screamed, "OH NO!!"

"What? What?" We thought he must've caught his foot in the spokes and was missing toes.

"I lost my shoe!"

"Your shoe?"

"Yeah, my shoe! Mom will kill me!"

"Where ya think ya lost it?"

"I dunno. Maybe back at the pool!"

A simultaneous, "What?"

We stopped. Yep, he was minus a little red tennis shoe. What to do. What to do? Well we couldn't go back to find it. No way. Crap. We may have left evidence. We'd get caught for sure.

"Gimme your shoe," Pat demanded. Tony handed it to him and Patrick flung it as far as he could into an alcove filled with tall weeds and briars.

"No one will ever find it there. No more evidence now!"

We raced home.

The next day, mom took us boys uptown to go shoe shopping. Tony's new tennis shoes couldn't be found anywhere and he had to have some for the summer. As we neared Tops for Shoes, Mr. Lowenberg intercepted us.

"Well, good morning Mrs. Landolfi. Doing a little shopping?"

"Hello. Well yes. We're going shopping for some tennis shoes for Tony."

"I see. Well, I may be able to save you some money… If they'll sell you a left little red tennis shoe – I'll bet I've got a right little red tennis shoe that will fit him perfectly."

Trouble With Girls

"Sir, yes, sir!"

"Is that so, you 100-pound draining pustule?"

"Yes, sir."

"Platoon, eyeballs! And just what window did you jump out?"

"The private's girlfriend's, sir!"

"Well, do tell, Private Romeo!"

"Sir, the girl's mom came home early. We'd skipped school and were making out when we heard the garage door open. The private had to jump out the bedroom window with only half my clothes on and run for my life…"

So went the retelling of one of my tribulations caused by girls. The drill instructor laughed and made me march up and down the squad bay for thirty minutes in only my boxer shorts, hunching the air every third step while saying, "Ohh baby, mommy's home open the window, I'm gonna jump." The rest of the platoon stood at attention, watched my stupid antics and tried not to snicker out loud.

So, yes, I've had a few scrapes with girls. Another favorite one was when Alice and I went for a walk down to the horse barn. When we returned, her mother was curious about the pasture and the horse. Her older sister was curious about Alice's shirt being inside out. We could have killed her.

And then, there was the time with Lyzza Boyle and Kimberly Whatsername. Kimberly's mom was a caterer and kept cases of Cold Duck champagne in her basement. My buddy, McCoy and I came up with a scheme to get drunk and lucky at the same time. We were fifteen and the girls maybe fourteen. We had skipped school and rendezvoused at Kim's.

Somehow we talked Kim into opening a case of bubbly. Have you ever drunk hot champagne? A whole bottle? It's nasty, but it does the trick. Well, about half way through our scheme, with our heads' spinning and the girl's inhibitions low, they got frisky. The only trouble was we hadn't decided on who was gonna do who.

Lyzza was skinny with freckles, scraggily hair and buck teeth, while Kim had a pretty face, was extra large, and had very hairy arms. I can still remember the moment that McCoy and I realized our dilemma. Lyzza had slipped her hand into McCoy's shirt and pulled him close with the other. His head jerked in my direction. Our eyes locked. Shock colored his face. He tried to pull away, but she was in mid-pounce, that handsome devil. The bottle of champagne found his mouth a microsecond before her lips. He drained it. Then, he got a kiss.

Kimberly followed suite. She embraced me and let go a big sloppy wet one that still makes me shudder. She had soft lips, I'll give her that and since she was twice my size, I went where she took me: the back seat of her mom's spare car. I don't know why we didn't go back in the house. We were drunk and nothing made sense anyway. McCoy and his girl took the front seat and we made out for what seemed like forever.

Once the girls had their fill of us, we escaped and staggered onto the golf course where we argued and fought about the injustices of our liaison.

Now here's another great memory. I lived in the basement when I was fifteen and I had another girlfriend named Alice, who lived about a half a mile away. We didn't see each other all that often, but every now and then she would knock on my window in the middle of the night. The first time I could hardly believe it, and every time, my adolescent fantasy mind went wild. From a sound sleep, I would hear tap, tap, tap. I'd pull back the curtain and see her smiling face. Incredible – now she was a great girlfriend. A guy's dream come true. No strings attached. Ahh, Alice – where are ya now?

The last one I'll tell you about involves that same basement bedroom. What a great room. The seventies were wild and I caught the tail of the tiger a few times. This time Natalie and Lisa had come to visit. We were listening to music and grubbing around. The door was bolted shut. Patchouli incense fogged the air and Led Zeppelin was rocking our world. It must have been too loud, or maybe mom thought the house was burning down.

Knock, knock, knock.

KNOCK. KNOCK! **KNOCK!!!**

"Michael? MICHAEL? **LOUIS MICHAEL**??"

We finally heard her. Oh my god! Oh crap! What should we do? I cut down the music.

"Hold on a second mom. The door's stuck."

I had to think fast. Jumping out the window would take too long and mom would probably see the girls roll in the yard.

An idea flashed. Brilliant!!!

Nanny's old refrigerator was in my bedroom because it fit. It was empty and unplugged, the girls were small. I shut them in and prayed that mom would be brief. I knew that there was a limited amount of oxygen in the fridge.

I opened the door.

"Turn down that music! What's going on in here? I thought I heard voices."

"Nothing, mom. I was just singing. Maybe it was too loud."

She stood in the doorway for about two minutes, hands on her hips, studying me, searching the scene behind me and listening for girl noise. Finally, she turned and walked away. I closed the door, bolted it and threw open the fridge. The girls were alive and laughing their butts off silently.

Those were the days.

Tonesha

Momma hollered, "Tonesha Dayon Gamble!! You bes' getchure nappy-headed, skinny black butt out dem bushes an in dis house dis very instant! …And Cornbread?! Getchure greasy, black hands out my baby's shirt and skedaddle 'for I get my shotgun and fill your Negro hide fulla buck shot!"

Mama was mad. I could tell 'cause she never called Otis "Cornbread" unless she was furious. That time, I think she woulda shot us both if she actually had a shotgun.

I'm fourteen and Otis is eighteen, he says. Mama thought he was more like twenty five, but I never would believe her. We was in love. Well at least I was. Otis was the most handsome boy around and probably the best kisser. Sandra Beal and Leona Washington had kissed him and said it was true. I hadn't never kissed a boy before, but I believed 'em.

I ran to the porch hollerin', "Mama, I'm sorry, I know it looked like Otis was tryin'…"

She said, "You hush up chile. I ain't hearin nothin' outta you. I'm too give out ta chase after yo mess. Get up ta ya room and wait till I calls ya. … Go on!! Get!!" and she smacked my rear as I ran by.

That was almost nine months ago and since then I ain't had nothin' but troubles.

Momma didn't hardly never fuss at me, but she nearly split my head open when she seen my baby bump. I lied and said I just been eatin' too much. But she said, "Tonesha, don't you take me for no fool. I know what I see and it ain't no eatin' too much. You been makin' on with Otis an now you's pregnant! I shoulda shot that boy first time I laid eyes on 'im."

I said, "No, mamma, no!"

She slapped my face hard.

"Hush up!" she said and din began to cry. "He ain't no good. He just like yo daddy, an every other black man, far as I can see. Jus' out fo' a good time. Then they gone. Sweet Jesus! Give me strength." She started to smack me again, but instead she hugged me so tight I couldn't hardly breathe. "An you still a baby yo'self."

Me and Otis broke up at the Patty LaBelle concert 'cause he got drunk and I caught him foolin' around with some white girl. He said he was just playin' to make me jealous so I would love him more, but I think he was just plain ole cheatin'. Then, he got mad 'cause I wouldn't drink none of that corn liquor he had. I done it once and he scamboozled me. I told him, "You knows I'm gonna have a baby and liquor ain't no good for babies."

Last month, Papa come by. I guess he heard the news an wanted ta see for hisself. He just walked up like he does, real slow and quiet. He don't stand up straight, didn't even say hello, only looked at me with bloodshot eyes and his crooked, gap-toothed smile, an' em long yellow teeth. He seen my belly and shook his head back an forth. He got such a sorrowful look, like he knowed what the rest of my life was gone be all about. I seen his face and started to cry. He didn't say nothin' only turned around and walked off.

It prob'ly wasn't a whole week before I heard that Otis had a accident. He used to work at the Tire Center changin' tires. But the machine dat twists the big metal bar around and gets the tire off broke somehow and it smashed Otis in the face. He's in intensive care right now, in a coma. They ain't sure if he'll make it. And even though I'm mad at 'im, I hope he does so he can see our baby.

Me and Momma been talking 'bout the baby. She been telling me how it's gonna be. She knowed 'cause she had her first one when she was only fifteen. I'll be fifteen in two months. Momma had me when she was almost forty and I'm her baby. I did have five brothers an sisters, but two's dead. Tyrell is in jail and Sereeta and Sherea went to Detroit. We don't never hear from them. I guess they's still alive.

Momma said I should give up the baby, to a nice home, says it'd prob'ly be better. The baby could grow up maybe with some rich white folks and not be poor like us. I cry just thinking 'bout that. I love my baby, but Momma's prob'ly right. I got no job an prob'ly won't never make no money, 'specially if I don't finish school cause of raisin' the baby.

All this worryin's drivin me crazy.

And now, if all that ain't enough, for days my belly's been a crampin' an hurting. The pains a been makin me cry. And yesterday, I started bleedin' down there an I'm afraid I'm gonna lose my baby. That's why I'm in this hospital bed right now. Sweet Jesus, give me strength.

Nurse, I'm sorry to be cryin and carryin' on so… and telling ya all this, but I ain't had nobody to talk to for a couple a weeks, ever since momma died.

Train Ride

One of my favorite memories is the time we snuck out after midnight, went uptown and climbed fire ladders on old buildings, then jumped from one to the other like in the movies. Another great memory was the time we crawled through a storm drain for a quarter mile with only one weak flashlight and no idea of where we were going. I'll tell you about hijacking the tractor or stealing a car some other time. This one's about hopping a train.

I don't remember why we were in Biltmore Village that particular day. Our usual M.O. was to meet, choose a direction and start walking, seeking challenges and adventures. We could wind up anywhere. Being young, foolish and still mostly cartilage, we would try most anything – especially if it tested courage and sanity and required unusual luck. We learned a lot about each other and ourselves. We particularly loved watching each other squirm while considering the test, knowing that failure meant certain injury, or maybe death. This day, we learned something important about Monty.

The train moves slowly through Biltmore Village, maybe 3 miles an hour. You can run faster and that gave us a great idea. Why not hop the train?

Everybody knows that you don't jump on the caboose, there's a guy with a shotgun and it's legal to shoot you. We hopped on somewhere in the middle, just ran along beside it, grabbed the ladder and swung up. Don't be shy, don't screw up, or you'll end up with no feet. All bilateral foot amputees lost 'em trying to hop a train.

Once on the ladder we scrambled up quickly, so the next guy could catch the same the car. We all three made it – McCoy, Monty and me.

"Yahoo!! We made it!"

"Yeah man! We really did! We hopped a train!"

"This is soo cool!"

On top of the boxcar, fifteen feet off the ground, we celebrated with high fives and laughed ourselves sick. We were outlaws, we were movie stars, we were heroes.

We watched the scenery go by. The train crossed the river.

Now, you might think that we weren't too bright, but it wasn't very long until we began to discuss the consequences of our conquest.

"Where're we going?"

"To the end of the line!"

"Yeah, the end of the line!"

"Where ya think that is?"

"I dunno. Maybe Johnson City, or somewhere."

"Huh, do ya think it'll stop before then?"

Monty, 13 and a year younger than us said, "Geesh, we'll be late for supper if we go that far and have to hop another one back."

McCoy knitted his eyebrows and said, "What if there isn't one coming back. We might have to thumb."

We all laughed nervously, hiding our fears of being late and in trouble again. The train picked up speed, 10 – 15 – 20, maybe 30 miles an hour.

"I don't want to go to Johnson City," whined Monty.

"Me either," said McCoy. "I don't wanna go so far we can't get back in time. My dad will kill me. He's still pissed 'cause I swiped his pistol."

"OK," I said. "But what'll we do? Jump? I bet we're goin' 25. Think it'll slow down?"

We all searched each other's faces for an answer: six adolescent eyes flooded with fear.

"What if there's a tunnel?" asked Monty.

The anxiety meter burst.

"We gotta jump! Watch for a good place."

We watched for a couple of minutes. Railroad tracks are laid on gravel beds and are lined with all sorts of trash, broken bottles, briars, barbed wire, and amputated feet. There was no soft grassy clearing.

"There's a spot. Hit and roll. Don't screw up!" ordered McCoy.

I went second and sprang with all my might. I like my feet. I rolled in the briars and broken glass and mostly missed the gravel. I was scraped and bruised, but alive with both feet. We all made it then, gathered together, high–fived and hee-hawed and prayed the caboose guy wouldn't shoot us. The train passed. There was no caboose.

"Now all we gotta do is get over there," McCoy pointed across the river.

We found a spot and started into the water. The French Broad is funky. It's muddy and smelly. I've never liked it and cringed when I waded in. I bobbed till it became too deep. After 10 yards I had to swim. The water was choppy and the current strong. It swept me downstream, but the others were close behind.

"Damn it, Monty! Whatcha doin'? Cut it out. You're gonna drown me!" McCoy screamed.

I turned to see Monty clawing his way onto McCoy's shoulders. It looked like they were both on the same pogo stick, disappearing briefly then barely surfacing enough for a breath. A fight ensued. It lasted the width of the river. Monty struggled to ride McCoy's shoulders and McCoy battled to get away. Both nearly drowned.

"What was that all about?" I asked once they were out of the river.

"He tried to kill me!"

"No I didn't. I forgot to tell ya I can't swim!"

The Maze

"All I need is a bandana and a cigarette," she said.

I was too drunk to offer a meaningful reply. Her lips elongated into a gorgeous toothy grin. I copied it, but I'm sure I looked stupid. I've seen photos of me drunk. An idiotic giggle bubbled up my throat. I couldn't stop it.

She slapped my face gently, turned and walked away into the midnight Utah desert. I watched dumbfounded as her untanned butt cheeks twisted to and fro with each step. In twenty feet she vanished.

When I awakened the campfire was out, a blackbird's caw tortured my ears, a mosquito feasted on my neck, my stomach boiled, and my brains wanted out.

While drinking two cups of strong black coffee, I surveyed the immediate scene: The Maze, a little visited area in Canyonlands National Park. It's remote, desolate, and the wildest place I'd ever been. All around were sculpted sandstone boulders and towering twisted walls colored yellow, orange, and brick. Long black stripes and splotches of desert varnish marred the cliffs as though paint bombs had exploded near their summits.

Finally, the caffeine hit, vision became clearer and curiosity pinched my swollen brain. *Where is that girl?*

I followed dents in the sandy trail up an escarpment and found her in a shallow cave. She was asleep, wrapped in an Indian blanket with camp gear and clothes heaped nearby and she wasn't alone. Another body was curled up in a similar wrap beside her. I couldn't see a face.

From twenty feet away, I watched the two for maybe five minutes. Then, a wave of guilt washed over me extinguishing my romantic fantasy. I felt like some perverted peeping tom. My face got hot. Silently, I turned and snuck back to my camp.

Just as I was shouldering my pack, I heard, "Where ya goin'?"

She was fully clothed this time.

"I'm headin' over to the Doll's House and Cleopatra's Chair, then wind my way outta here up toward Goblin Valley."

"Why don't cha come with us? We're going pretty much the same way?"

I followed her back to the cave. Her name was Jasmine. Her companion, Terra, was her sister. They were on a hiatus from college in Berkeley. Both were philosophy majors and were seeking "inner peace and enlightenment" a' la Timothy Leary and Carlos Castaneda while roaming the remote desert southwest.

As they explained their purpose and journey thus far, I was hypnotized by Jasmine's eyes. Terra's were beautiful too, but Jasmine's eyes were like nothing I'd ever seen; they were penetrating, sensual, and almost violet. They were as wild as her story: peyote and mushroom adventures into the mind while meditating for hours with rainbows and fireworks and the vibration of the Universe pulsing through their brains.

We explored the desert and each other for four more days. I doubt your imagination could paint a picture anywhere close to our reality during those hours.

We parted, promising to stay in touch, to rendezvous someplace wild like Telluride in the winter, or Yosemite next spring. We wrote letters for a while, but we never crossed paths again.

One day, long after I had ceased being obsessed with her, a postcard arrived. The photo showed Ayers Rock in Australia. Written on the back was, "Our son is 5 today. He loves you. You'd be proud. Love Jaz." There was no return address. A vacuum drained my heart.

Years later, I was at the Telluride Film Festival with my wife, enjoying a pint of a local micro brew. The town was crowded with the rich, famous and beautiful. The patio bar was bursting with excited patrons discussing films, possibilities, and adventures. Two tables away a riotous group of twenty-somethings whooped it up with toasts and teasing and shouted stories. I overheard one ask another about his youth in Australia. His answer took a while. I watched intently and listened as best as I could through the cacophony. The kid was tall with features like mine. His shoulder length hair was blonde and his eyes were nearly purple. I was mesmerized.

"Utah, that's the wildest story I've ever heard," a redheaded girl shouted. "I don't believe a word of it!"

"It's true! You can ask my mom. Well, ya can't right now cause she's floatin' the Green, then she's heading to the Yukon for a month."

The void in my heart from long ago stirred and pulsed with excitement. Could this handsome youth with violet eyes and an adventurous mother be my son?

The crowd surged and interrupted my view. When it thinned, the young man was leading his group out of the bar. I struggled to catch him, but the throng was thick. I caught up at the red light. He was riding shotgun in an open jeep.

"Hey, Utah?"

He turned and flashed a Hollywood smile.

"Yeah, man! 'Sup?"

Our eyes locked. The light turned green and the jeep began to roll.

"What's your mom's name?"

"Jazzy, man! Jazzy!"

He disappeared with the traffic. My heart emptied and then… burst with pride.

Robin's Ruin

I walked in just as she said to Sharon, "You wonder why? It's because that's the way I see the world… and because of my family."

"Whatcha mean, your family?"

"Oh, shoot. They're all white trash."

"What?"

"That's right – from way down in Alabama. Not a one of 'em works and I'm always having to send 'em money."

"What on earth for?"

"They're idiots and ne'er-do-wells. They're all crazy. That's why I'm always broke and workin' my butt off with all these twelve hour shifts. They're constantly asking for money to fix their old junkers, or get outta' jail. The latest one was Ronnie needing $3,000 to get out on bail cause he stabbed my sister-in-law in the neck. I told him he's goin' to prison. I'm not sending him any money."

"Stabbed her in the neck? You've got to be joking!"

"No I'm not. He's my half-brother, but I'm not sending him another dime. Last year he was busted for selling meth, but he got off because of some technicality. I gave him a thousand bucks for a lawyer and told all of 'em – this is the last time I'm comin' to his rescue."

"Golly! I thought my sister getting divorced and needing a place to stay for a few weeks was bad enough."

"Oh, honey. That's just the tip of the iceberg. Over the years, my sister – the hooker – has needed bailing out a half a dozen times. One time, her kids and ex-old man stayed with me for almost a year. They're the reason I left Alabama. The bums! I didn't tell 'em the lease was running out and the day it did, I had the movers come, pack my crap, and I disappeared while they were all at a movie."

"No way!"

"Yes, I did."

"Where'd you go?"

"That time I went to St. Augustine, until Joey showed up."

"Who's he?"

"My nephew. My sister's kid. He was runnin' from the law and hid out in my storage unit for about a month, till the cops caught him."

"How'd they find ya, the rest of your family I mean."

"Well, I had to stay in touch with my mom, 'cause my father was really sick then. He's dead now, but before long everybody got my number from my mom, or my good sister."

"How many of ya are there?"

"One mom and one good sister, but she's trailer trash, too. She can't help it. It runs in the family. Then, I've got the whore sister and two half-brothers and about fifty nieces and nephews, all of 'em on welfare and thieves. They'd steal the gold crowns outta your mouth if you slept too soundly."

"Well, Robin, do you think they're just using you 'cause you've got a good heart and a good paying job?"

"Well, daaah – of course they are and they're gonna burn in hell, sister!"

"Wow! Well, why do ya let 'em do that? And why's the good sister trailer trash?"

"Aah, come on – I'm just as stupid as they are and Cherry Anne is trash 'cause she never finished beauty college. She got pregnant and had four kids. And now she's divorced for the second time, can't find a job, and only likes unemployed drunken slobs for guys. Yeah, but she must do somethin' right 'cause she's had about a dozen of 'em. 'Course they're all bums and they drink and …"

"Oh, come on. Really? I thought she was the good sister."

"She is. She's good to momma and her kids. She's just stupid. I mean she doesn't use her head right."

"I've got a brother kinda' like that."

"Well, I pity you then. Right now she's living at mom's 'cause they got evicted. The bum she was with was raisin' Cain in the trailer park and threatened this skinhead neighbor with a baseball bat. Oh, I forgot to say that the bum is black. Anyway, they got kicked out and now she and all those kids are back at mom's. And mom is eighty-four and lives in a single wide in Mt. Vernon. It's crime city USA and hot as Hades!"

"Robin, this is all terrible. No wonder you moved to Asheville."

"Yeah…. Crap! I gotta go! My break is over. I gotta get back, I'll see ya next week. I start vacation when I get off."

"That's nice, sounds like you could use it. Where ya goin? The beach, I hope."

"Naw, I'm goin' to mom's. The air conditioner don't work and her car was repossessed. My sister's car is shot and the kids need back-to-school clothes. I'm gonna go down there for a couple days and see if I can help."

No Chevy

"I ain't gon ride in no Shivolay!"

So we walked – all the way to Smilin' Jack's Seafood-N-Hushpuppies in Surfside, about three miles.

"Why won't cha ride in a Chevrolet?"

"Cause ma daddy never did. He would drive a Merkurry, or even a Buick, but he always said that a Shivolay was for commoners. And we wasn't no commoners."

I had to agree. She was not common.

I was proud of my brand new El Camino convertible. *It* was beautiful, but *she* was gorgeous. I let the insult slide. We'd met at the cotton candy stand beside the pier. She agreed to have dinner with me, but wouldn't tell me her name. Every time I asked, she only grinned and flashed incredible hazel eyes.

As we walked, she read aloud what the different signs said.

The third time I asked her name she read, "Sweet Tea," and said, "You can call me Sweet Tea. I ain't gonna tell ya ma real name till I figgur out if I like ya, or not."

It was certainly not common, but I went with it.

She ordered the Captain's Platter. It was a huge pile of everything.

"How ya gonna eat all that?"

"I ain't. I just like the boiled shrimp… well and a few hushpuppies."

"Huh? Well, I don't mean to pry, but why'd ya order it, if you knew you weren't gonna eat that much?"

"Oh. Well, mamma always said if a boy was taking ya out, ta order the most expensive dish on the menu and drink water with a slice of lemon in it."

"Oh."

"Yeah, that way he knows ya got expensive tastes and the water 'n lemon shows ya got couth."

I smiled and watched her squeeze lemon into her water glass. I wasn't entirely sure what couth was, but I bet it wasn't common.

After the meal, we sat on the beach 'til almost dark.

"I gotta go now, since it's dark," she said.

I offered to drive her home.

"Oh, that's alright. I only live around the corner from here. I'll just walk. It'll be alright." She stood up and left.

"Hey, Sweat Tea! Ya gonna tell me your name?"

Over her shoulder she giggled, "Maybe tomorrow, if I see ya and ya buy some more cotton candy."

I thought about her for almost three miles as I walked back to my car. I couldn't stop grinning. She was the most uncommon girl I'd ever met. The next day, I bought some cotton candy.

At the end of summer I returned to school. A week later, I came home one afternoon and found Juanita sitting on the porch of the farmhouse I rented.

"Daddy don't like it, but I told him I couldn't live without cha. So he brung me up here." She smiled as bright as the sun. It was the most beautiful thing I'd ever seen.

We were together for sixteen years and daddy was right – nothing about her was common. Every day with her was fresh. She was innocent and enchanting, sensual and whimsical. She loved motorcycles, but wouldn't ride on one.

"I just like the sound of 'em. Rrummrumm. And all that power they got. It's kinda like bein' a cowboy in modern day times."

And she had to have fresh flowers; giant white lilies were her favorite. They lasted for days and the fragrance was hypnotic.

She didn't care about money. She'd spend it if she had any, or could live forever without it. She loved puppies and would hug and pet and gush all over them, but never wanted one of her own. Sometimes she'd sleep till late afternoon and sometimes she'd be up before the birds, taking a hot bath with a dozen scented candles burning.

In 1973, we went to a peace rally in D.C. A bunch of us were arrested, handcuffed, and taken to jail. When 'Nita saw that she would be riding in a Chevy paddy wagon, she raised such a fuss in front of a news crew that the cops let her go. We laughed about that a million times.

And years later, after our car was stolen, she sat on the curb and absolutely refused to get in the rental car the insurance company sent. I had to explain to the agent that 'Nita was very particular.

"Please send a Buick, or Cadillac. I'll pay the difference if I have to."

"Sir, I can't do that."

"Then, we'll have to walk. You can cancel our policy."

We moved to the mountains and settled down in the country. We had a nice house and a garden. I worked and she stayed home, like in the fifties. We never had kids. So we had the time and freedom for romance and fun. We showered each other with love. Life with 'Nita was beautiful.

In 1986, 'Nita became ill. She was diagnosed with breast cancer and it had spread to her brain. She was constantly nauseated and in the end couldn't walk. The last few days she was delirious, either talking nonsense or unable to respond. I was holding her when she died.

The most uncommon thing about 'Nita was that she never told me she loved me. I guess it was supposed to be understood. With her final breaths, she rallied and said, "Sweet tea? Don't cha never forget…" she gasped for air and I began to cry figuring what she was about to say with her last breath.

"I love you too," I whispered as she struggled.

"I ain't gon ride in no Shivolay."

Blackout

His first memory was more visceral than visual. There was the faded image of his mother's face, twisted in pain, eyes red, and swollen. Mascara stained her cheeks. Her face was large in the picture; they were nose to nose. The sensations from that moment were razor sharp, his chest heaved, ragged halting breaths, his young mind boiled like copperheads trapped in a bucket of bleach.

"Shut up! Shut up, you little twerp!" she yelled in a whisper. "If you don't, I'll beat your whining little butt, and Simon will probably kill us both!"

Nicholas Black was four years old. His mother died that night.

Life in his aunt's house wasn't much different, except there were more kids, more men, and more alcohol. His mom and her sister were almost twins; they both attracted ill-tempered drunks who used them for short periods, abused everyone, and either left in a rage or were carried off by the police.

Nicholas' childhood was miserable. It was filled with violence and fear. Happiness and self-worth never bloomed, his psyche poisoned daily by hatred and cruelty. He ran away when he was fourteen and felt lucky to be alive.

"Where'd ya go, Nick?" the suit asked in a calm low pitched murmur. He pushed another steaming cup of coffee across the steel-topped table and offered another cigarette. Nick accepted both.

"California, Hollywood."

"And you were fourteen? That musta been scary. How'd ya get there? What'd ya do for money? Ya stay with relatives?"

It was 2:30 am, Nicholas was exhausted. His neck hurt from being cranked by the big black cop, and his wrists still complained. The cuffs had been so tight and the edges were sharp.

"I thumbed, got rides with truckers mostly, but one old couple took me a long way."

"What about money and a place to stay?"

"I did what I had to - stayed in shelters and other places."

"What'd you do, steal some here and there, and hook a little?"

"I'd rather not say. Why's any of this important? What're ya getting at?"

The detective calmly stated, “Just trying to get to know ya, Nick. You know, trying to get a feel for who ya are and where you came from.”

Two-thirty in the morning was no time to think. All the questions and digging for memories made his head throb. His memory was shot, the worms of alcoholism had long ago bored holes in his brain. Retrieving memories was like scooping water with a sieve. He’d been having blackouts for years; sometimes he could pull up a memory, most were vague and some didn’t exist at all.

“So, ya don’t recall how ya came to be in your ex–wife’s house with her blood all over ya and your prints on the murder weapon?”

“No, sir, I swear! I started drinking around noon and I kinda remember goin’ over to Nancy’s house, but I do that a lot. I walk by and stand outside and imagine what’s going on in there. What kinda games my kids are playin’ or TV shows they’re watchin?”

“Well, the neighbor lady saw ya hiding in the bushes, watching the house. The next thing she knew, there was a scream and you were going in the house. She called 911 and they found you crumpled in the corner, crying and blood-soaked, your wife and kids dead. I find it hard to believe ya can’t remember slicing your wife’s throat and stabbin’ your kids to death.”

Nicholas sobbed into his cupped hands, slobber and tears mixed with blood, a pink pool of pain dripped from the table onto his ruined blue jeans.

He spent two nights in a cell with six other men, the next three in the infirmary with his wrists and ankles lashed to the bed. The DTs almost killed him, seizures, sweats and violent outbursts challenged the strength of the leather restraints. Sedative injections helped a little. After that, a suicide watch isolation cell was his home for six weeks.

Finally, he was marched before a judge to witness the latest evidence. The victims had been making a home movie using their laptop’s video camera. The kids were acting out a scene from Harry Potter, and mom was the referee of the Quidditch match.

It had taken the cops six weeks to retrieve the footage because the laptop had been badly damaged during the melee. The final scene captured the murders. The children were playing, one sprang back screaming. He toppled the computer, the room cartwheeled, the picture played sideways. A man's blue jeans appeared, his fist gripped a knife. Nancy fell with the blade plunged into her neck then, her chest – four, five, seven separate times. There were screams and blood everywhere, the children ran, plead for mercy. Nicholas watched in horror. None of this was familiar. *Damn blackouts, damn memory*. Then, just before the screen went black, the man's face appeared.

Nicholas lost his breath – the murderer's identity was indisputable: Nancy's first husband Steven Smith.

Jack Ruby

Merriam Goldstein had been a victim all of her life. She was born into a Catholic family and dubbed Merriam Samara Deaver. Merriam as a tribute to her grandmother and Samara is Latin for "protected by God." But God failed her.

Merriam was first victimized by her mother, who had little tolerance for her fourth child. She cried too much and so received severe spankings and long periods of isolation. Next, she was a victim of the hateful nuns at St. Theresa's School for Girls. Then as a budding teen, she fell victim to her uncle's advances and lost her virginity, her dignity, and her faith. She never breathed a word about that terrible night and she vowed to never be a victim again.

Merriam became known as Sam during her early adult life. She thought a change would do her good. She met a man. He was handsome and charismatic. He had been in the war, an Army captain and decorated hero.

Levi showered Sam with love and attention and never worried about religious differences. He was even fond of JFK. He voted for him and supported the young president's decision to invade Cuba. The couple stayed glued to the TV news during JFK's assassination coverage.

"There should be more Jack Rubys in this world," Levi told Sam when they watched the video of Oswald's murder. He went on to say, "More men should stand up for their beliefs. Sometimes you have to kill the bad guys."

Levi embodied integrity and pride. And he became a successful gunsmith. His custom firearms were prized by the best marksmen in the country. He taught Sam how to build them and how to shoot weapons of every kind.

Sam and Levi were married for almost sixty years when he died in 2006. They had worked hard and made lots of money. Levi had wisely invested the majority with a financial wizard, almost two million dollars. He died knowing that his precious wife would live comfortably for the rest of her life. But in 2008, the wizard's magic was discovered to be a scam; Bernie Madoff went to jail and Merriam Samara Goldstein lost her fortune.

Last year, she had to move into a crappy little rental in Jersey. She was 81, alone and almost penniless. All that remained from the couple's hard work and success were some photos, her memories, and a few of Levi's guns. Every day she missed her husband, and every day she cursed Bernie Madoff.

Last month, Sam nearly fell victim to the "Grandma Scam": the one where someone calls an old lady pretending to be her grandchild falsely jailed in Haiti and needing several thousand bucks for bail.

She was in the process of sending four grand when a store clerk alerted her to the possible scam.

"Better call your grandson and find out," she said, "before ya wire the money."

She took the advice. He was home and safe. She was grief-stricken at the thought of being stupid and gullible and victimized yet again.

Yesterday, when the door bell rang, Sam found a kind-faced young woman and a clean-cut young man who were selling cleaning products. They talked fast, not giving Sam a moment to refuse their sales pitch. Their van was left running at the curb.

"Ma'am, our product is the first industrial strength cleaner approved for home use and if you'll allow us to clean a small area of your floor. I'm certain that you'll be amazed."

"Well, I…"

"It'll only take a second and I know you'll be pleased."

The two squeezed inside. The girl began spraying the floor and the guy scrubbed. They chattered incessantly and worked for about five minutes, never giving the old woman an opportunity to interrupt.

"Well whatcha think, ma'am. Pretty nice, huh?"

"It's so easy," the girl chirped. "And affordable."

"You can buy the product now or we can come and clean for you every week. It's your call," said the man.

"Well, I don't know. I'm a …."

"Wait a minute lady. We just cleaned your whole floor and just look at it."

"It was pretty dirty," said the girl, "and now look how that old tile shines."

"Well, I don't really have the money for it right now. I'm…"

"Aw come on, now. I bet you got the dough and it's not that much anyway. And, if ya can't afford the product or our weekly services, the least ya should do is pay us for our time."

"Well I…"

"Yeah," chimed in the girl. "We did a nice job and saved ya a day's work on your hands and knees."

Sam felt her face flush. She was being hustled, victimized again. When will this stop? She hated the feeling.

"Well hold on. Let me get my purse, just a minute."

The couple flashed grins at each other when Sam turned away. Their scheme had worked again – another easy robbery, bolt to the van and tear off down the street with her money, cards and identity.

It took a couple minutes. The safe was locked and the dial resisted arthritic fingers. Sam returned with her purse.

"Alright. Now, let's see. Where is that…? What do you two think you should get?" She pawed through her purse.

"Well uhh, how about …," the young man began.

Bang! Bang! ... Bang! Bang!

They each got two bullets in the chest and died on the clean tile floor.

The Tractor and the Buick

I've told you that we were rambunctious and that our idea of fun involved adventure, challenge, and usually mischief. By today's standards many of our exploits would be considered criminal. In the early '70s, kids got away with more. Parents and cops were more inclined to understand and forgive impetuous pranks.

Remember the story about hopping the train and swimming the river, the one where Monty nearly drowned? Well, three weeks after that escapade my brother Patrick, Monty and I were snooping around the Grove Park Inn searching for anything exciting. We found it in the form of a tractor.

"Look at that. What the heck is it?"

"Huh? I dunno," said Pat.

"It's a street sweeper. That brush twirls round and round," I replied.

"I love tractors. Let's see if it'll start up."

We piled onto the John Deere. Patrick nabbed the seat. We all three grabbed the steering wheel and yanked it back and forth while making tractor sounds like 5-year olds. Pat attacked the pedals and shifter like Richard Petty gone berserk. Monty and I elbowed each other for next turn.

"Where's the key, ya see the key anywhere?"

"Ah, they ain't gonna leave the key out here."

The commotion simmered down while we searched.

"Naw, but what about this?"

I found a cotter pin and it fit into the ignition. The lock turned.

"Press in the clutch, Pat."

I twisted the makeshift key again, the engine roared to life and the sweeper began to twirl.

We were astonished. We whooped and shouted and laughed like lottery winners. Patrick got so excited that his foot slipped off the clutch pedal. The engine stuttered. The tractor bucked. It was in second gear and it took off. We cheered louder and slapped each others' shoulders.

"Where we goin?"

"I don't know."

"It don't matter, drive on brother. Let's go!"

We could run about as fast as we were going and it was a good thing. In about 50 yards we heard, “Hey, you boys! Stop right there! You stop right now and bring me back that tractor!”

“Oh crap!” yelled Monty. “Whadda we do?”

“Jump and run! Leave it goin’. He’ll have ta chase it – not us!”

We leaped off and rocketed away with the man shouting at us, but chasing the tractor. We escaped and steered clear of the Grove Park Inn for a while.

Two weeks later, Monty and his family went to the beach, Patrick had a great idea.

“Ya know that old car of Monty’s dad’s?”

“Yeah, what a piece of crap.”

“Yeah, but you can start it without a key. I’ve seen his dad do it.”

“You’re kiddin’! Let’s go!”

The Buick was unlocked and started right up. Pat got to drive first ‘cause it was his idea. He headed up Macon, past the tractor spot and up to the Parkway. Being short for twelve, he had a hard time seeing over the steering wheel, but he did a good job, nearly wrecking only a few times. I drove next, down Elk Mountain and into north Asheville. Merrimon Avenue was busy and scary. I was fourteen and had only driven with my mom on Sundays in the empty mall parking lot, never in traffic. We survived my near misses.

McCoy took the wheel after we stopped at Burger King. He drove through town, the windows down, spirits soaring. We were the bravest: heroes, movie stars, gangsters. Our grins could barely fit in the car. Intoxicated by audacity and seated in the proof of our foolishness, we stopped at several popular hangouts to show off the stolen car. McCoy added to our clout by flaunting the pistol he had secreted away from his father, a deputy sheriff. Everyone was impressed, even awed. We were crazy, the wildest kids in town, the coolest.

McCoy cruised through the neighborhoods and back up the mountain. We felt untouchable, unstoppable. It was the best day of our lives. We zoomed down the road with the radio blasting and we were going too fast. We passed the tractor spot again and approached the 90-degree turn. Fifteen miles an hour warned the sign, we were going 45.

“It’s the bad curve, McCoy,” I cautioned.

"Slow down, McCoy! It's the bad curve!!" Pat screamed.

"What?"

In unison we shouted, "It's the bad curve!!!"

McCoy jammed the brakes, the bald tires stopped spinning, the car slowed some. He jerked the steering wheel, our path curved a little, but not enough. We slammed into the pine trees and skidded along them making the turn. When we came to a stop, Patrick and I sprang out of the car and bolted down the street. McCoy was trapped, his door crushed shut. Pat and I hauled ass and heard McCoy calling after us to return, promising torture if we didn't. Reluctantly, we did.

The front tire was flat, the driver's side ruined, fluids were leaking and the front axle broken. It made a horrible noise, but we were able to drive it the two blocks necessary to return it to its parking place. We fled like escaped death row inmates.

Yeah, we got caught. And that's another story.

Bobby Morgan

My favorite prisoner was Bobby Morgan. In 1977, he was a sailor onboard the USS Independence – CV62, an aircraft carrier. He was in the brig for the heinous crimes of missing too many musters and failure to comply with an officer's orders. What that meant was Bobby slept late too often and wasn't at his duty station on time. He was a low energy kinda fellow and even though he was directly ordered to show up on time every day, he just couldn't seem to do it. So, Boatswain's Mate Seaman Morgan was sentenced to ten days in the brig.

I was nineteen years old, a corporal and in charge of the brig. I ran a tight operation, but tried to help the prisoners improve themselves. These were kids just like me, no serial killers or career politicians. I was tough, but honest and compassionate. In fact, I was too compassionate according to my CO. About two months after Bobby was released, Captain Newman fired me for letting the prisoners pray one night before going to bed. I wanted to ask him about the 1st Amendment, but figured I'd regret it.

Anyway, I met Bobby when his Chief Petty Officer brought him to the brig. His sleeves had no stripes, but his wrists had handcuffs and his ankles were connected by chains. He smiled brightly as he was handed over. I guess he thought he was going to be on a ten day vacation. He was wrong.

Back then, Marines guarded all shipboard jails, or brigs. The day shift guard took his post at 0430. At 0435, the prisoners were gently awakened as a metal trash can lid was repeatedly bashed against the cell bars while the sentry screamed an explosion of curses and threats. Only launching jets made more noise. Bobby did not sleep late.

After reveille, the brig rats made their bunks and cleaned the area as though the President would be inspecting the cramped metal prison. Scrub brushes, Ajax, Pine-Sol, Brasso, toilet brushes, toothbrushes, and rags scrubbed and shined every square inch until it was totally spotless and basically sterile. One speck of dust or spot of anything, even in the toilet or on the shower floor, would send the entire group back to work. I doubt Bobby had ever worked so hard and certainly never so early.

The predawn cleaning was followed by one hour of exercises, and they were hard core. Groaning or complaining only bought more torture and if everyone wasn't sweating profusely, we would do bends and thrusts or mountain climbers until I was exhausted. Then, my charges ate breakfast Marine Corps style, sitting at attention, in silence, eyes forward, bite and swallow. Ten minutes max. At 0630, they were loaned out like library books to Navy Petty Officers for work details, returning to the jail just before supper.

Bobby failed to return one afternoon, but came back the next.

"Where ya been, Bobby?"

"I'm so sorry Cpl. Landolfi. I know I gotcha in a lot a trouble, but I just had to have a beer." He had taken a liberty boat into Naples, Italy and spent the night drinking.

I hoped it was good beer because he got a court martial, thirty days of solitary confinement in a five-by-seven cell and thirty days of bread and water – for real, only bread and water. He could not be loaned out for a work detail, or taken to exercise. His only time outside the cell was to potty and shower. He lost a lot of weight even though I brought him all the bread one tray would hold three times a day.

One day I found Bobby crying. He was pitiful, like he'd just run over his own dog.

"What's the matter, Bobby?"

He wiped his nose on his sleeve and said, "Cpl. Landolfi," he snuffled three times. "I just heard Elvis died!"

That evening I sprinkled a little sugar on his bread.

After his sentence ended, he found me on the mess deck.

"I just want to thank ya, Cpl. Landolfi, for treating me fair. I've learned a lot from you. And I wanna show ya somethin' cool if ya got a couple minutes."

"Thanks Bobby. Okay, I've got a few minutes, but I really shouldn't be hangin' out with an ex-prisoner, ya know."

He led me to a compartment filled with bombs, crawled up on one and patted it, signaling me to sit beside him. I did.

"I'm getting a dishonorable discharge and I'm shipping out tomorrow. I sure appreciate all your good advice and trying to straighten me out and your good example and all. You're a strong leader and the other brig rats think so, too."

He shook my hand and grinned. Then produced a hand-rolled cigarette, lit it, and tried to pass it.

"Bobby! Are you nuts!? We'll both be in solitary forever!"

"Aw, they won't catch us…"

"No, cause I'm outta here. Good luck, Bobby."

I flew out of that compartment, but looked back as I closed the hatch. Bobby remained astride the missile; his eyes sparkled like a kid's on Christmas morning. He was grinning ear to ear, holding his breath in and still trying to pass me the joint.

Kelly and Me

"Ya think I could be starting into menopause?"

"Huh? What, just because you're always tired, irritable, and mean?"

"Yeah."

"You been like that since I met cha, twenty years ago."

She quickly twisted a towel and snapped my bare butt. I'd just gotten out of the shower.

"You dirty rat!" She snapped at me again, but missed. I ran into the children's room and leaned heavily against the closed door.

"Ya gotta come out sometime," she said. We both laughed like little kids.

In the kitchen, she warned, "You're drivin' me crazy."

"I know. That's my plan."

"Well ya better stop, or I'll come up with a plan of my own and you'll be sorry."

"I'm already sorry. Why ya think I'm aggravating ya all the time? I'm trying to get you to kick me out so I can give ya half of my stuff and start a new family, have six more kids and a new crazy wife."

"You've got it. I'll sign the papers this Friday."

"Why wait till Friday? So you can get my paycheck?"

"So you can take out the trash Thursday."

We drove to the grocery store. No, she drove. She won't let me drive, I'm unsafe.

She turned on the radio, "Country 103.6 – music with the most twang in the mountains!" And she turned it up loud.

"What're ya doing? You don't even like country music and it's way too loud!"

"What? I can't hear you. Whadya say?"

I turned the volume down.

"I said it's too loud and ya don't even like country music. Are you trying to kill me?"

"No, I'm tryin' to drive **you** crazy. If you don't jump out and kill yourself, I'll have to go to Plan B."

"I doubt I'm goin' ta jump out at thirty miles an hour. What's Plan B?"

"I'm gonna poison ya to death."

"Ha! Now that's funny, you been tryin' to do that for twenty years, every suppertime."

"Ha ha ha. Very funny. I have not. It just so happens I'm a lousy cook. This time – if ya don't jump right now – I'm gonna poison ya with something that's undetectable. Even CSI won't be able to figure it out and I'll get off scot-free. I'm gonna find it on the Internet and it'll taste good. You'll love it and you'll die real slow, it'll take weeks. You'll slow down more and more and finally you'll just stop."

"Can't you make it quicker? I'm ready right now…"

"Then jump!"

"Not at thirty. I don't mind dying, but I don't want to be all busted up."

She slapped my left knee hard and flashed her Cheshire cat grin. We both laughed, but was she serious?

In the store, she sent me for milk and bread. I found her in the household items aisle. She was reading the ingredients of ant control powder with Acephate and had lighter fluid and kitty litter in the buggy. The hairs on the back of my neck bristled. We don't have a cat and I hadn't seen any ants lately.

"Whatcha doin?"

"Oh, picking up some stuff for mom and Mrs. Strupp."

"So…. I guess the cat's got ants and you're gonna burn 'em out?"

"Somethin' like that."

"OK, 'cause it looks to me like you're buying ingredients for a yummy poison dinner."

"Oh pooh. I wouldn't buy 'em right in front of ya. I'd be sneakier than that."

"Would ya, now?"

She grinned again. Just so happened her mom did have an ant problem and Mrs. Strupp was out of cat litter. The lighter fluid remained a mystery.

Two nights later we argued. I cursed, she cried. We went to bed in separate rooms. We tried to make up the next day, but ill feelings remained. We spent the whole day in a funk. At supper, she tried to lighten the mood, but I was too tired to be teased. We slept in the same bed, but as far away from each other as possible.

I came home from work early the next day. I had vomited twice and felt terrible. I retreated to my bed and buried myself under the covers. I felt chilled and then too hot. I sweated and shivered at the same time. I just wanted to die.

This went on for three days during which time Kelly was sweet to me and fed me lime Jell-O and cinnamon toast. Did I taste antifreeze in the Jell-O?

On Friday morning, while my wife was at work, I asked my mom to drive me to the doctor. He poked and prodded me, listened to my chest and drew a blood sample. In the end he declared that I had the flu.

"Whew," I said to Kelly. "I thought I was going to die. Didn't you?"

"Well, I was a little worried. And I'm glad you're gonna live. I really do love ya and I'd surely miss you."

She folded my hand in hers, squeezed it tight, and we laughed like only best friends can.

Nightmare

God abandoned our small town while Satan attacked with bullets and bombs, spraying the blood of our children on classroom walls and in carnival-colored stairwells. Two hundred twenty nine children lost their innocence and thirteen lost their lives as guardian angels, patron saints, good luck charms, and cosmic sanity turned a deaf ear.

We were a couple of hours into an extremely dangerous craniotomy when we got the word. The news couldn't have come at a worse time; Dr. Silver had begun to unwrap a massive brain tumor that was strangulating crucial and sensitive blood vessels. A slip of the knife or a miscalculation would mean certain death. The distraction was unavoidable and devastating. Silver put down the scalpel, pushed away from the microscope, and stared slack-jawed as the charge nurse delivered her message.

"Dr. Silver, staff members, I'm sorry to interrupt, but this is extremely important. I'm informing everyone that a horrible tragedy has occurred and we're all going to be effected. There's been a shooting at the middle school and police are on the scene right now. The school is on lock-down and so are we until we know about casualties. We're also canceling the rest of today's elective cases."

"Sam, you've got to be joking," Silver replied.

"I'm afraid not and if there's any way to finish quickly, or suspend the rest of this case, ya need to."

"There's no way I can do that."

"I understand. And I need to know if any of the rest of you have kids at the middle school?"

Sheila dropped her pen, fell into a chair, and replied, "I do. My twins are in the sixth grade!"

Her face was ashen and eyes wide with panic. "Sam, I need to leave. I need to find out if they're okay."

"Sorry dear heart, nobody's allowed to leave. We're locked down."

"You mean I can't go find out about my children?"

"I'm so sorry. We all have to stay put to help manage this disaster."

"Well then, I quit! My kids are more important than this job!" She snatched down her mask and threw off her gloves.

"Security isn't letting anyone out and is turning away all visitors. Take a deep breath and go get a drink of water. Call the school, then come back and help wrap this thing up."

Sheila stormed out, our collective hearts dropped. My stomach twisted; my kids were in that school last year. Silver sat dumbfounded. We all watched each other for several moments. The implications of impending carnage sent fears ripping through our guts. Gunshot wounds to children, bullets in heads and chests, death, destruction, madness and murder. Where is our God, our children's protector?

Sheila returned more panicked than when she left, "The phones are all busy, even cell phones won't work right now. The news says there's so many calls the cell towers are overloaded. There's a news crew at the school showing students being escorted away, but there's a bunch trapped inside and the shooter is still loose! He's still shooting at random, even at the cops. And two bombs have exploded! They don't know who's been hurt or killed." Tears rolled down her face.

Silver pushed away again and turned to look at Sheila. The strain in his eyes reflected her fears; she was his favorite nurse. Without words we all got back to work.

The phone rang. Sheila hit the speaker button.

"Room one, Sheila speaking."

"Sheila, get out here now!" ordered the charge nurse.

We all stiffened and watched Sheila race out the door. In ten minutes she was back.

"The news showed all the kids lined up at the evacuation relocation site so parents could see their kids. Emily was there, but I didn't see Sarah." She reported while wiping her eyes.

"Are all the kids out?"

"No, there's still fifty-two missing along with four teachers. They've already found six children dead and thirteen wounded!"

"Oh, my God," said Silver.

Sheila collapsed into her chair and held her head in her hands. Tears fell so heavy with worry I thought they'd go straight through the floor. We pressed on.

Two hours later the phone rang again, speaker on, "Room one, She…"

"Mommy!"

"Emily! Where's Sarah?"

"She fell on the stairs and I lost…"

The connection died. Sheila stood paralyzed, tears poured. Within the hour the surgery finished. As we were leaving the room, Sam called over the intercom, "Sheila?" We heard chaos in the background. "Sheila, your child is in the E.R. I don't know her condition, but when you finish get over there, stat."

We delivered our charge to recovery and ran to the Emergency Department. We burst through the doors, voices shouted and nurses scurried, mayhem ruled. Trauma teams worked frantically in several rooms. We saw dead children. No one could help us. We searched the bays.

"Mom!"

"Sarah! Oh my baby!" Sheila shed the most joyous tears of her life. "Are you alright? I was so worried that you mighta been…"

"I'm OK mom. I just broke my arm, that's all."

Dr. Gross

"Dammit! Arrgghhh… gaww…dammit!" groused Goodman Gross and he pitched the overhead light as though in the major leagues. It swung away in an arc, then violently crashed into the other ceiling-mounted surgical light and tilted, blinding me with fifty-four high intensity LEDs.

"These lights suck! Everything around here sucks. It's all a bunch of crap!" the orthopedic surgeon barked. He focused the remaining lamp. We eyeballed each other. No one spoke. What a way to start the day.

Usually, a surgical suite is one of the most controlled places on earth. Pandemonium erupts only during extreme resuscitation efforts, and the surgeon usually is helpful during the chaos, not the cause.

This day, orthopedic surgeon Goodman Gross had stomped into the OR in a bad mood, spewing his foul-mouthed, deprecating sarcasm and confirming his reputation as an immature, irritable, egotistical prick.

"Come on you slackers. I've got nine cases and a soccer game at seven. No time for idiotic chit-chat, or lame-assed questions. Get movin' and get me a second room with a crew that's smarter than you brainless bumpkins. Let's go!"

He grabbed the light's handle, adjusted its position and started to call for the scalpel when the light drifted. That's when he pitched the light, cursed and fumed about everything sucking. I rearranged the light that was blinding me and watched the reactions of everyone else. They were frozen.

"Scalpel… cautery… suction. The suction's not working. Sheila, some moron didn't hook up the suction again."

"I'm sorry, I'm afraid that moron was me."

In a flash she connected the suction, but it wasn't very strong and Gross let out a string of expletives and stomped his feet like a three-year old. He breathed deep and counted to ten.

"I don't have time for incompetence."

During the next twenty minutes, Gross blasted the scrub nurse mercilessly because the scissors were dull, the drill's battery was exhausted, she gave him the wrong suture, and the X-ray tech wasn't in the room.

The X-ray tech took her time setting up for a shot and Dr. Gross lost it. He dropped the "F" bomb and threw a screwdriver at her and burned holes into her with an enraged stare.

Everyone in the room was dumbfounded. Sheila and I spoke at the same time.

"That's enough Dr. Gross. Just calm down." Sheila ordered. My message was the same.

"Like hell I will. Get that woman out of my room and get me some equipment that works. Call the charge nurse and get me somebody that knows what the hell they're doing. Now!"

Sheila made the call, not for better help, but to report Gross's behavior.

"Dr. Gross, I think you need to simmer down and take a break. Your behavior is unacceptable. You cannot throw instruments," said the charge nurse.

"I will not simmer down and I will not take a break. I do not have time for this bull. You'll take this stinking crew out with you and get me a new one stat…"

"No sir. You'll hold your tongue and your temper. Sheila, I'm calling security."

"You will not! And whatcha think they'll do anyway?"

"Sir, I'm going to have you relieved. Sheila, phone his office and get the on-call surgeon over here to finish this up."

Dr. Gross leaned against the anesthetized patient and froze. I'm sure that behind his mask his mouth dropped open. I watched his eyes widen with disbelief. Hate shot out of his pupils. Looking into them was like peering down the bores of a double barrel shotgun; they were hollow, black and dead. They belonged in a mental ward.

When security arrived the surgeon went berserk. "Get outta my room right now!" he ordered.

"No sir, you're gonna put down the knife and take a little break."

The guard moved toward Gross.

"If you try to touch me I'll slice this bitch's femoral artery!"

The guard called for back up and took out a Tazer.

"Calm down doc. We don't want anybody hurt now. Just put down the knife and step away from the patient, please." He took two steps and aimed the Tazer.

The next moments were a blur. Two more guards blasted through the door with Tazers drawn, the first guard made another step toward the surgeon. The scrub nurse shrieked and hid behind her hands, Dr. Gross cursed and raked the knife across the patient's groin, arterial blood geysered, the surgeon spun, grabbed the scrub nurse and held the scalpel to her throat.

"I'll cut her head off!"

Her knees buckled, he twisted trying to keep hold of her. The guard fired, the Tazer prongs found Gross' face. He fell forward in an electric seizure cracking his head open on the floor. Sheila pounced on the patient's groin and slowed the bleeding. Blood pooled under Gross' face. The guard cuffed the surgeon's hands behind his back and then rolled him over to find that the scalpel had sliced deeply into his neck.

Dr. Gross didn't die, but he did suffer a massive stroke. Now, he's in prison, paralyzed and wheelchair bound, wearing a diaper that's changed when the guards have time.

Pickups

When I finished recounting the one about meeting this beautiful chick in Spain, getting drunk and lucky, and … robbed, Celeste told how she met her first girlfriend.

She giggled – she was halfway through her third beer, "I was at this rest stop outside of Atlanta, taking a pee when someone went in the stall beside me. She closed the door and peed like a fire hose, really loud and for a long time. Then, she cussed and said, "Hey, you next door. Ya got any toilet paper to spare? This one's all out."

I said I did.

"Can ya hand me some?"

The stalls were solid from floor to ceiling. I told her she'd have to open her door. She said it'd be okay. So, when I finished I opened her door to give her a big handful. I almost died, I couldn't believe it – she sat there bare-chested with her jeans around her ankles!"

The guys all chorused, "No way! Oh my god! What happened next?"

Celeste grinned like a Cheshire cat, "We hit it off and were a couple for about a year."

"Details! Details!" demanded my buddies.

"Naw. You sickos'll just have to use your imagination." She laughed, missed her mouth and spilled beer all down her shirt.

Ben was next.

"Dude, you won't believe this one and it's all true! I was driving back to Virginia and stopped to get gas at this little place in South Dakota. It was one of those funky joints ya find out west. You know, a gas station, bar, laundromat and casino all in one – in the middle of no freakin' where. Well, I was sittin' at the bar sippin' a brewsky when this gorgeous chick sits beside me and starts flirting. She had jet black hair and mocha skin and knockers out ta here." He demonstrated and smiled with huge drunken eyes. "Man, she was sweet! Anyway we shot the bull for a few minutes and then she asked if I'd like to jump in a natural hot springs, that her dad had one on his property not too far away. Well, hell yeah!"

We all laughed and sat forward to hear what insane predicament Ben was getting himself into; he has that kind of reputation.

"So I buy us a case of beer and tell her which truck is mine then, I go take a leak. When I come back out to my rig she's already downed three beers and was getting smashed. I got back on the interstate for about ten miles, then hopped off where she said to. By then she'd downed two more and was getting frisky, rubbin' my leg and talkin' dirty. She whispered the directions in my ear and then stuck her tongue in and groped me. I almost wrecked! Then she scooted way over against her door, opened another beer and watched me drive. Dude! I drove and drove and thought I was goin' where she'd said to, but after about fifty miles on these godforsaken dirt roads I asked her where we were. She says she doesn't know – she thought I knew. We stopped at this skanky dive in the middle of BFE and she went in, I figured for directions. It was another of those nasty bar and casino places on the outskirts of the reservation. She'd said white guys weren't very welcome so I waited. And waited and waited. Dude, it was takin' way too long and just as I decided to blow her off and burn outta the parking lot, guess what happened?"

We were all dying laughing and each guessed something ridiculous.

"Ya got four flat tires."

"Indians came out and beat the crap outta ya."

"The cops came and gotcha for drunk driving or kidnapping."

"Her dad showed up."

"Naw, even worse!" Ben said. "You'll never believe this. Dude, I heard a baby crying! It was in my truck, behind my seat!"

I fell out of my chair laughing.

"Oh yeah, oh yeah! A baby about a year old, wrapped in an Indian blanket! No stuff. I about crapped my pants! Where'd it come from? I guessed it was hers and she'd put it in my truck while I was pissin' and it'd been asleep the whole time! Dude, it was so ridiculous!"

"Well what'd ya do?" asked Kayser. "Leave it on the door step and haul ass?"

"No man, I picked it up and went inside. She'd been in there probably half an hour. And guess what?"

"No freakin' tellin'"

"She was sittin' at the bar with a liquor drink almost empty…AND… directly behind her, you ain't gonna believe this, was this skanky stripper chick swingin' around a pole!"

We cackled, slapped our knees and couldn't wait to hear what happened next.

"She was so tore up I don't think she recognized me. I asked her about the baby and held it out toward her. Her eyes popped open when she realized what was going on. She had forgotten all about her newborn. Then she got pissed at me, gave me the stink eye, cursed me and yelled something in Lakota, I guess. She snatched the baby and tried to slap me, but fell off the stool and rolled on the floor. I went to help her, but two big drunk Indian dudes pushed me away. One said I'd better haul ass. Said whitey's gonna lose his hair if … and I didn't wait for the end of the sentence. I burned rubber."

Adventures with Freddy – Part One

Freddy was our next door neighbor. He was from way out in the country and he was totally wild. He had adopted my brother Patrick as his workmate, playmate, and accomplice. Patrick was that kind of kid: everyone's best friend and mascot. I tagged along on occasion.

Freddy was in his early thirties when he loaded Patrick and me into his beat up International Harvester truck and hauled us down the river to where he had grown up, "Bloody Madison."

Our first stop was Riverbend Billiards. It was a dismal cement block building whose tin roof was so old it was rusted and curled on the edges. It had prison bars on all the windows, a massive bulletproof steel door, and an indestructible padlock protecting it.

Inside was dim and smelled of unwashed hard-working, chain-smoking, whisky-drinking, godless farmers. The barkeep nodded at Freddy, but no one spoke to him. Patrick and I were very self-conscious, he being 12 and me only 14.

Freddy laid a dollar on the bar; he was given a beer and a rack of balls. He broke and Patrick shot next. Their game lasted about ten minutes, during which Freddy washed down the beer with two shots of tequila. It was a friendly little place until one of the regulars challenged Freddy to the next game. After another tequila, the match was on.

The two played six games. Freddy won five, and a dollar with each. In the end things got rough: too much liquor, too many lucky shoots. Banter turned into an argument and everybody balled up their fists. We were asked to leave. Pat and I were happy to go, though we said that we'd've killed the sorry bastard if he'd started to win the fight.

Unfazed, Freddy drove on.

We crossed the French Broad, tilted around a hundred sharp curves nearly killing granny at her mailbox, Elmer Fudd on his tractor, a three-legged dog, and ourselves. We headed towards Sandy Mush, an area well known for rednecks, moonshine, and shotgun murders.

Freddy turned onto a nearly hidden gravel drive and gunned the engine, spewing rocks and dust onto the main road. He whooped like a victorious Apache and slapped his knee so hard he cursed in pain. The worn out truck fishtailed and smacked into a barb wire fence, knocking a post over. My brother and I locked eyes and nervously laughed as we bounced around in the cab. This was before seat belts. The obscure track led to a ramshackle farm house: the old home place.

Our guide stomped on the brakes and we piled out. The abandoned clapboard building sagged in the middle. It seemed exhausted; five generations had "growed up here" and had used it all up. Kudzu and hornets claimed it now. We peeked in the windows, at the shed, and where the still used to be while being told stories of Freddy's childhood.

Next, we headed back toward Marshall. He took the curves a little slower this time. I guess he'd sobered up some. Freddy stopped at his old buddy's house, said his name was Winston Churchill and that he made the best moonshine in the state. Pat and I locked eyes again, giggled and wondered if we'd live to tell this tale.

Churchill was having a party. Freddy joined in pitching horseshoes and sipping moonshine. After God knows how much corn liquor and losing several rounds of horseshoes, Freddy challenged everyone to a knife throwing contest. A drunken Freddy and knives, even dull ones, seemed a bad idea.

Fortunately, the game didn't last very long. Freddy kept losing, got mouthy and mean. Before a fight could break out, Churchill suggested we leave. Freddy cursed his friend, but finally relented. He promised to return, win the game, and reclaim his money. He fell getting into the truck because of a muddy shoe with no traction and a drunken grip on the steering wheel. He lay sprawled on the ground for a minute then, popped up, hopped in, and took off at top speed before closing his door.

The only reason we lived through this escapade is because halfway down the driveway Freddy had to pee. When he got out he fell again. This time he couldn't get up without our help. He was so drunk that he agreed he couldn't drive. Patrick and I had done a decent job driving the stolen Buick a few weeks before, so we talked him into letting us drive. We hoisted Freddy into the bed of the truck. He couldn't even sit up.

The International was much harder to drive than the Buick. The steering was imprecise and the clutch so stiff I could barely press it in. The brakes were shot and scared us to death. Freddy slept throughout the trip. We parked a block from our house so our parents wouldn't see him in such condition or me driving. He was sound asleep, curled in a knot with a logging chain for a pillow. He wouldn't wake up. We covered him with a tarp and told his wife where he was. She hoped Jesus would take care of him, 'cause she wouldn't.

The next morning, his truck was gone. His wife said he was up in Madison with his chainsaw, no tellin' when he'd be back.

We wondered how Churchill and his buddies were doing.

Adventures with Freddy – Part Two

About a month after showing us his old home place, Freddy decided to introduce us to some new friends. We again drove through Marshall and way out into the boonies. Almost in Tennessee, Freddy pulled off the blacktop and onto another nearly hidden single-track gravel road. In a couple hundred yards, an old rusted stock gate forced us to stop. Freddy dialed the combination on the big brass lock and swung open the barrier. Patrick lurched the International forward in the wrong gear; it bucked and hopped and the engine nearly stalled. Freddy relocked the gate and had to run to catch us.

We drove through the oaks and poplars over a ridge and down into a holler where we paralleled a creek and passed into a rhododendron tunnel. It was shady, cool, and musty. After a quarter mile, we gained a rise and saw our destination – an old farm house with two grain silos.

We could hear *Stairway to Heaven* playing as we parked in the yard beside a half dozen other junkers. Folks sat around the porch on a tattered sofa, a couple of rocking chairs, and on the steps. They were friendly and relaxed, smoking cigarettes, burning incense, and drinking iced tea. The odor was not only tobacco and jasmine. There was a guy holding a banjo and plucking notes in time with the Zeppelin song. He smiled and greeted us warmly. His name was Blue Sky Rider, Freddy's newest best friend. They hugged and we were introduced.

"Sky," as everyone called him, led us on a tour of the place and explained who he was, his philosophy, and the workings of the farm. He had been a lieutenant in Viet Nam and had seen too much meanness and killing. He had become disillusioned with the government and had begun to learn Eastern philosophy. Now, he hoped to help folks become enlightened and ease their suffering through meditation, communal living, and chemistry.

He asked my brother and me what we wanted to be when we grew up, and he advocated us being chemists. He said that everything: the earth, the moon, the stars, the entire universe, including ourselves, were the result of chemistry. Energy became matter and matter became different elements which bonded together to become everything in the known universe. Chemistry formed us and it can improve or destroy our world. He was fanatical about the subject. Pat and I agreed to become chemists.

We walked through the house. Heavy curtains sealed the living room's windows and there was a black light suspended from the ceiling that caused anything white to glow. It sent posters of *Easy Rider* and Janis Joplin into spacey action. There were couples on bean-bag chairs making out and the room was thick with smoke; we began to feel happier. We watched the posters for a few minutes, then Sky moved on.

We lost Freddy somewhere between the kitchen and the backyard. Out back under a huge oak sat a guy and several girls. He was playing a sitar and chanting some mantra. He sat on an old cushion, totally naked with the instrument covering his delicate parts. The notes he plucked resonated with an off-key twang that buzzed and held onto the air. It seemed a reflection of everyone's state of mind. Sky was impressed and sat lotus style while we listened for what felt like eternity. We were then shown one of the silos.

They were both made of fieldstone and had tin roofs. Sky thought they were probably a hundred years old. The one on our right was padlocked. We weren't allowed in there. He showed us the other. It was three stories tall and divided into three floors, with ladders leading to the upper floors. The top floor was an observatory with two big telescopes and maps of the heavens. The middle floor was a sanctuary where folks could meditate in relative silence, the thick stone walls repelling rock music and barnyard commotion. The ground floor held farm tools and bushels of potatoes and beets and vegetables, all kept fresh in the cool dark room.

In between explaining things, Sky kept jabbering about chemistry. He was a chemist – not by training, but by trade. Everything on the farm relied on chemicals, mostly natural, and they all benefited the group in various ways. They were healthier because of healthier food and they were happier because of that and a special elixir he produced.

It seemed true; everybody we met had a rosy complexion, was laid back, and smiled a lot.

We hadn't seen Freddy for a while and asked Sky about it. He smiled as though he knew a secret. We began a search, went through the house and the barn, stirred the chickens around, and looked in the well.

We finally found him behind the barn, buck-naked in the hog wallow taking a mud bath and singing, "…We all live in a yellow submarine, a yellow submarine, a yellow submarine." He said he'd burned his clothes, then burst out laughing like a pack of hyenas. Sky said he'd be alright by in the morning, but we couldn't wait that long, we needed to get home by dark. Reluctantly, Sky gave us a ride to Marshall and we thumbed from there.

Freddy showed up two days later. We were surprised he was alive. His wife wanted to kill him, we wondered what had happened and he couldn't believe we'd left without him.

Adventures with Freddy – Part Three

Freddy was a hard worker: manual, back-breaking, sweat-soaked, filthy-handed, mindless toil. He excelled at picking up heavy objects, chain-sawing things to pieces, and dragging almost anything with his beat-up International truck and a huge logging chain. He was a hard drinker, always distilled spirits like Jack Daniels, Jim Beam, or crystal clear moonshine from Madison County. He also played hard and, like all rednecks conceived by a fourteen year old in the back seat of a Dodge, born in a taxi cab idling in the 7-11 parking lot while the driver bought her cigarettes, and toothless by age 27, Freddy's play always involved gas-powered motorized toys and lots of alcohol. He liked to get drunk and pretend his truck was a race car or a rocket ship. He'd drive through the woods at top speed knocking over small trees and launching off of dirt mounds he'd built. Once, he had a backwards race in the Santeetlah Lake parking lot. The Corvette beat him easily and he almost got killed; his miserable brakes failed and he stopped only because he wrecked into a concrete picnic table that broke to pieces and wedged in his wheels.

And of course, all self-respecting boys from Madison County must clean their pistols while drinking. "And ya gotta keep 'em loaded – just in case."

Freddy was a proud man and wouldn't take any guff. He was always ready to fight, especially if he'd been drinking. He was a redneck's redneck, professing to be against everyone not born in the mountains and anyone more tan than himself. He flew his redneck flag by keeping the crappiest house in the neighborhood, a washing machine on the front porch, a dilapidated sweat-stained sofa under a tattered blue tarp in the side yard ready for cookouts, more kids than you could count, and maybe a half dozen vehicles in various stages of disintegration heaped here and there.

He only wore plaid flannel shirts, Wrangler jeans, and steel-toed work boots, and was never without Black Maria brand chewing tobacco. Only sissies went for Redman and Levi Garret; Black Maria was the real deal, for real men. It came in a small brick wrapped in wax paper. I tried it once, bit off a plug, chewed it twice as directed then, tongued the wad between my teeth and cheek. It was the vilest thing I'd ever tasted. Rotten opossum guts couldn't have been worse. My heart rate tripled, my head about exploded, I spit it out almost immediately and wanted to puke for twenty minutes. Freddy shook his head in disgust. I was obviously weak. My brother chewed it and grinned and spit. Patrick was the real deal.

Freddy had moved to town hoping to improve his life, but country bumpkin genetics and alcoholism created hurdles too tall to overcome. He was also accident prone: falling out of a tree chain-saw in hand, landing on his head on the pavement, a couple of broken ribs and chain-saw lacerations needing two dozen stitches, but he was lucky that time.

Another day, he was splitting firewood the old-fashioned way, hoisting a gigantic maul high above his head and slamming it down into lengths of oak and locust. All went well until he swung the tool too close to the wire cable clothes line. It didn't break. The cable acted like a rubber band and propelled the maul back to crush Freddy's face. He was a sight: a black and blue face with a broken nose, cheek, and jaw. He would've broken out teeth if he'd had any. He needed surgery, but wouldn't go to the hospital so he lived the rest of his life with a warped face and a bulldog underbite.

You won't be surprised that Freddy died young, or that alcohol and hubris were involved. Detectives investigated the accident scene, interviewed the parties he'd been with that night then, reconstructed what they believed happened and told his wife.

Sometime around 3 A.M., Freddy crashed into two telephone poles, snapping the first one at bumper level and bending the second to resemble that tower in Pisa. The truck stood upright on its headlights, Freddy hung upside down out the windshield. He probably died on impact. His blood alcohol was three and a half times the legal limit. He'd been at an acquaintance's playing cards, drinking heavily, and winning.

As usual when Freddy was drunk, an argument erupted. He was accused of cheating and he countered that everyone else was lying. The game ended. For some reason Freddy gave the guy who was angriest and the biggest loser a ride. Maybe each planned to fight the other. The telephone poles ruined any schemes of a scuffle and the accident became an opportunity for the survivor to reclaim his money. A bloody hand print marked the passenger door handle and a trail of large crimson drops led away from the wreck. No winnings were discovered in the truck, Freddy's wallet was empty and his passenger never found.

We followed along on Freddy's final adventure – to the graveyard, watched him lowered into the ground and covered with dirt. It was a pitiful affair; there were only six mourners, seven if you count the preacher who'd never met Freddy. We wished him good-bye and good luck then, Patrick and I drove out to "the old home place" where we toasted our crazy friend with two slugs of moonshine apiece. As we left, I stomped the gas pedal and spun the tires just like Freddy would've. We whooped and laughed like idiots and drove home telling and retelling stories of adventures with Freddy.

Mind Bender

The belt was too tight, it pinched me. I'd've complained and loosened it, but not in the present company. It'd be too wimpy and besides I was afraid to move. I'd never been more terrified – not jumping from the train, or off the 80-foot cliff, or even crashing into the trees in the stolen car. This escapade was beyond crazy. I couldn't believe what I was doing. The needle was coming fast.

"Just a little pin prick and there'll be no more pain, but you may feel a little sick," Doc quoted Pink Floyd and chuckled.

I couldn't take my eyes off the needle and held my breath. The hollow spike pierced my arm. Doc tugged the plunger, gently mixing my blood with the solution in the syringe. Our eyes locked, he grinned.

"It's in." He pressed the plunger then, released the tourniquet.

The drug smashed into my brain. Lightning flashed, thunder exploded, machine gun hail and hurricane winds attacked from within and wanted out. I tasted strong chemicals. Satan's vacuum stole my breath, vision faltered. Sparklers and whirligigs spun along with laughing rainbows. Sound warped, stretched, strobed. Reality ripped apart. My chest collapsed. I soared on angel's wings, then gravity pressed me into the sofa, no – through the sofa. From the ceiling I watched my body dissolve and drain onto the carpet. Life was over; I was free. I saw God.

"Take a breath, dude," Doc urged. "Don't forget to breathe! Breathe, breathe, breathe," his voice echoed. He shook me violently and slapped my face. I inhaled. He smiled; that made me feel better. He was a professional, a medical student – knew what he was doing, even had a leather bag with sterile syringes and alcohol swabs. I was safe. He'd been doing the same bag for days and knew how much to use – its strength was known. The couple with him said it was the best stuff they'd ever seen, straight from Sicily, from the Mafia.

The orgasmic tornado lasted only minutes, and then a slow motion pleasure cruise sailed me around the cosmos. Unimaginable bliss engulfed me, soaked through my skin, washed my brains in thick, warm peace, even love.

A sultry current lifted me from the carpet into outer space. Particles from the Big Bang vibrated through my body and Jupiter flung me to the edge of the universe. Soft maternal fingers caressed my face. Sound returned and brought the words of Dylan's sour voice, "I came in from the wilderness, a creature void of form…" I blinked out of existence, tumbled head over heels, then reemerged honey-sweet and swollen with joy. This is how life should be. I never want it to end.

The girl was next.

"A little more, a little more. That's how ya fly, that's how ya die," she giggled as she held out her arm.

She took a shot twice as big as mine, fell back into the chair, drooled and grinned with wild animal eyes. I watched everyone else shoot up, their eyes roll back inside their skulls, lungs collapse, and balance fail. Their smiles ricocheted off each other. It was like a movie projected on the living room wall. I had to watch, I couldn't move. Breathless tranquility bound me in place.

In the wee hours I found a comfortable spot beneath the kitchen table and slumbered until sunlight attacked from around the edges of heavy curtains. I found my brother curled in a ball beside the toilet and nudged him with my foot.

"It's morning, let's get outta here."

The other three were in the living room, the couple entwined on the sofa and Doc slumped in a chair. The room was dim. We tiptoed to the front door. Patrick inspected Doc.

"Mike!" he whispered loudly. "He's dead!"

The needle was still in his arm, poisoned blood dried and black in the pit of his elbow. He was cold and wooden. Patrick bolted to the door.

"No! Go out the back!"

We were out the back door in a flash.

"Wipe the handle, look both ways, run through the woods."

We sprinted. Bushes and briars snagged our clothes and ripped our flesh, impeding our escape. We stepped into an alley.

"Don't run. It'll look suspicious."

We covered our faces with our hands and quick–stepped away.

Through the years we'd sought mischief, invited trouble, and courted disaster, but no one had ever died. For weeks we wondered when the police would crash through the door with pistols drawn and cuffs ready. But they never did.

My wife proofread these pages and with every sentence her face grew redder. When she finished, she crushed the pages and hurled the wad at me. Tears fell.

"I can't believe you were so stupid!" she bawled, then spun around and stomped away.

"Hey! Where ya going? Don't get mad. None of that ever happened. It's total fiction."

Fist Fights

In case you were wondering, I can tell you from experience that it's not a good idea to punch a magistrate in the face. Now, I wouldn't have hit him had he not been coming at me with his fists all balled up. Hey, I was already having enough trouble with the other guy who was trying to beat my brains out.

I guess I should start back at the beginning, so you'll understand how I got into such a mess.

My best friend McCoy and I joined the Marine Corps together. We went to boot camp together, but were separated after that. About a year later, we met again in Newport News, Virginia, and celebrated like young marines do: we drove around in his car and got drunk.

Our last stop was at a bar where he thought we'd have fun. Unfortunately, we were kicked out immediately, not for misbehavior, but for failing to follow the dress code.

According to the little lady who twirled us around and pushed us back out the door, my Hush Puppy shoes and McCoy's black Billy Jack tee shirt were offensive. We wouldn't fit in with the drunken patrons or the strippers. I don't remember being obnoxious, but I'm sure we questioned her edict. In any event, we were sent packing.

My next memory is of us driving out of the parking lot and a huge bearded guy glaring at us from the club's doorway. He shot us the bird. I said, "Stop the car, I'm gonna kill 'im." McCoy did. I jumped out and bull-rushed the six-foot four, three hundred pound barroom bouncer and we went at it.

Most likely he was winning, but I don't remember being hit. I do remember ducking a mean right hook and coming up to see this gray-haired guy running at me with his fists balled up and murder in his eyes. I smashed his face with a killer right of my own and watched him drop, he was out cold.

The next instant, I was face down in the parking lot, two big men were stepping on my wrists, one of them figured I needed to sample the pavement for taste and texture.

It had started raining, so I got a little sup of gritty water as I inhaled and asked the nice policemen to please stop grinding my face in the puddle and breaking my arms. The diligent officer kept his knee on my neck, the pressure monitor in my cheek said he weighed 257 pounds. My arms were cranked behind my back and metal cuffs were clamped on as tight as humanly possible. I was yanked into a standing position.

We were pitched into the back of a squad car and given a nice ride uptown.

I hate handcuffs; they're uncomfortable and humiliating. I get depressed every time I wear them, but even worse is the sound of an impregnable steel door slamming shut and locking. The hopelessness you feel is unrivaled in normal life. You ain't getting out 'til they let ya. It was a lonesome and worry-filled night curled on the concrete shelf. I had no pillow or sheets, only ten other unwashed desperados smelling of cigarettes and alcohol. They all snored violently.

I spent three long days with my new best friends. McCoy was in a different cell and got out the next morning. His captain musta liked him better than mine did me.

What a great experience – NOT! It cost me a thousand bucks and a delay in promotion, and of course, I didn't learn my lesson.

Months later, McCoy, who was stationed in Newport News, told me that he had met other marines with the same story as ours. The magistrate owned the club, the bouncer exercised his middle finger often and young leathernecks paid a lot of money to the city of Newport News.

Yes, I've been in a few scuffles and I'll tell you about one more.

I was involved in a small riot in Naples, Italy. Yeah, we were drunk, but we weren't purposefully hurting anything. My friend Maxie, a man of color, and I were uninterested in walking across the street and shopping for Elvis-on-velvet paintings, or fake Rolex watches, so we leaned against a Fiat and waited on our buddies. The next thing we knew, we were attacked by a horde of diminutive, middle-aged Italian men.

They fussed and yelled at us, but we couldn't understand a bit of it. We did understand being punched in the face. Back to back we slugged away at our attackers. I became surrounded by a mob of soft-fisted guys who pounded my head. I didn't fall, so one of 'em bit my arm with all his might. It left a scar for years.

Our buddies rallied to our defense and the melee exploded into a riot. Pint-sized Italians were swarming us like Amazon army ants on a honey-coated caterpillar. They tried to kill us with anything they could find. One had a razor edged harvesting scythe, another found a baseball bat, a third swung away with a car fender. The madness went on until a Marine guard broke it up. He gave his night stick to Maxie and called the Shore Patrol. Our boys began to turn the tide now that we were armed. The civilians scattered when the Shore Patrol arrived. No one was seriously injured, but the Marine guard got in trouble for surrendering his weapon. He was court-martialed and we had to testify against him.

Uh oh, my five minutes are almost up. So, I'll have to tell the rest of this story another time. But, I will tell ya the ending. To go to the court-martial we were launched off of an aircraft carrier in a propeller-driven mail plane.

Perfect Alibi

My wife is clever. She found a way to kill me without implicating herself.

"I've got somebody who wants to fight ya," she said, studying my face for a reaction.

"Oh, really? Why's he want to fight? Ya make him mad or something?"

"No. He wants to box ya. He goes to a boxing gym and can't find any sparring partners."

This sounded kind of ominous. Was this guy such a monster that no one with any sense would get in the ring with him? Turns out he had been in the Army and wanted to fight a Marine. I fit the bill so I gave him a call.

I love to fight, in the ring that is, and at 49 I was still full of piss and vinegar. And that summer I was trying to show my 19-year old son that it's okay to take chances, to jump into the unknown for the adventure and experience of it. Here was a great opportunity to demonstrate that even though you know you'll get hurt, it's okay to take risks. We set up a meet at a gas station close to the gym.

It felt kinda like a drug deal. We pulled up in our respective trucks and met halfway, shook hands, exchanged pleasantries and I followed him to a nearby building.

When I got back in my truck, my boy said, "Dad, did you see that guy?"

"Well, yeah. I talked to him and shook his hand."

"Okay then, good luck."

I could almost hear the gears in Ryan's head telling his brain what a fool his father must be and that I was about to be murdered by this guy who was 15 years younger and 50 pounds heavier. I hoped the gears were wrong.

When we returned home, Ryan entered first. I was a few steps behind. Kelly sat in the family room, the other kids in her lap. Neighbors had popped in and out, and she had made several phone calls during our absence. She had the perfect alibi – phone records and eye witnesses.

Ryan had a black eye, crusted blood around one nostril and a few dried red drops on his shirt. I waited in the garage for a few seconds.

"Oh my God! What happened, Ryan? Where's your dad!? Is he dead?"

Was there a note of satisfaction and accomplishment in her voice?

"No, he's not dead. He's coming…"

I stepped in.

"Oh my gosh!!! Honey!! What on earth happened? Are you okay?"

Was there a hint of disappointment?

"I'm fine, just a bruised and bloodied nose."

"Is that all your blood on that shirt? It's ruined! Don't you touch any of my furniture!"

"No. That's Chris's."

Ryan explained what had happened, "Dad met the guy at the gas station – he's a monster! Then we followed him to the gym and warmed up on the heavy bags and speed bags. We jumped rope and did some pull-ups until the other guys in the ring were finished. Then, we wrapped our hands and put on head gear and gloves. Dad went first. You shoulda seen it! Your guy was huge and dad is old and scrawny, but he's got a good left jab. When the bell rang, dad didn't dance around like some fighters do at first. He went right at the guy and jabbed, jabbed, jabbed. Poor Chris didn't even fight back, well maybe a swing or two, but by the third jab his nose started bleeding. In about a minute dad musta punched him fifty times and there was so much blood pouring out that the coach made 'em stop. He told the guy he had to go outside and bleed in the dirt, not on all his equipment."

Kelly's eyes were wide, "You're kidding."

"No, I'm not. It was like a chain-saw massacre. There was blood everywhere, all over the ring, all over the gloves and all over dad! Then, the coach made me and dad fight, first with only our left hands. That lasted almost a whole round until dad smacked me with a right hook."

"I forgot, I guess. It's just natural to use both hands. It was a reflex. Sorry."

"Yeah, right. Well, then we went at it with both hands and we both got bloody noses."

"Well, was it worth it? Did ya have fun?"

"Yeah, and I learned why 50-year olds shouldn't fight 19-year olds – they hit too hard."

Ryan beamed with pride and said, "And I learned to never fight dad. He doesn't fight fair."

"Hey, I didn't mean to forget. Plus you got me back."

Then I said to my wife, "And there's a lesson for you, too."

"What's that?" she asked.

Next time ya plan to kill me, better get a guy with a gun."

Run Ins

The last time I almost got shot, I was 49. It had been a while since I'd been threatened with a gun so I was out of shape, reflexes a bit sluggish. But like all the other times, I was minding my own business.

I was showing my oldest son Summit Lake and recounting adventures with the rope swing and diving from the train trestle. It had been years since I'd been to the lake. The swing was in a different tree, but it was spectacular.

We made a couple of jumps each. Then Ryan decided to go higher. He carefully climbed a cartoonish ladder made of rotting planks, thick sticks and a paint bucket nailed to the tree. I watched in silence, the capricious affair just as likely to disintegrate as not. He reached a decrepit platform twenty feet up, turned to look at me with a tentative grin, caught his breath and froze. At that moment, I suddenly felt a presence to my right.

"Looks scary."

"Yes it does," I replied without turning toward the voice.

"Ya know you're trespassin'?"

I twisted my head and found I was shoulder to shoulder with an armed railroad policeman.

"What? No, I didn't see any private property signs."

"Didn't ya come across that trestle?"

"Yep."

"Well, that's railroad property and there's a sign. Burlington Northern has the right of way through this property, a hundred feet on either side. You're trespassing and I suggest you leave." He turned toward me and stroked a holstered pistol.

Ryan watched motionless.

My mind screamed, "You've got to be kidding!"

I'm not very good at being threatened, never have been. So, I turned to face the guy, put my left knee directly in front of his jewels and readied my right arm for an uppercut. I had to tiptoe a bit to place my nose four inches from his. Then, I said in a soft deadpan voice, "Some friendly information. I'm an old Marine Corps assassin, killed three men I know of and my conscience doesn't bother me. If you decide to pull that pistol, you'd better kill me."

I turned away and said, “Ryan, you take a couple of turns and I’ll take one. Then, we’ll leave.”

Dick Tracy vanished.

The next to last time I almost got shot was by a South Carolina Highway Patrolman. That time, I had just pulled out of a peach stand and was getting up to speed when the blue lights came on. I pulled over, the cop walked up to my window.

“Sir, ya know ya’s speedin’?”

“No sir, I didn’t. I may have been doing fifty but the sign down there says 55.”

“Ya ain’t there yet. It’s 45 here. I gotcha at 57, at’s 12 over. Lemme see yure license and registration.”

I complied, but my wife and her mother began to argue, demanding to see the radar printout.

“Ma’am, I’m not showin’ you nothin’. Don’t have to.”

“You do in Ohio,” Libby said.

“This here’s Sow Ca’lina, ma’am.”

He wrote out the ticket and handed it to me with a smirk as I started the car. I was fuming. He was such an ass.

As I took the citation I said, “Sir, with all due respect… you are a liar.”

He stiffened, then got twitchy and slapped his holstered pistol a couple of times.

“Turn it off! Turn it off now and get out of the VE–HICK–EL! Get out of the VE– HICK–EL now, boy!” He grabbed at his pistol and jumped around like Barney Fife. I laughed.

“Whatcha gonna do, shoot me?”

Kelly smacked my head.

I turned off the truck and got out. He demanded I get behind my truck where it would be difficult for my family to see, but directly in front of his dashboard camera. I stood at Marine Corps attention absolutely motionless and silent while he circled cursing and threatening me. It didn’t work. I didn’t move. If he beat me senseless, the video would prove that I had not been a threat. When he was exhausted he let me go. I marched back to my truck and left without another word.

The first time I almost got shot, I was 15 and cutting across Mr. Lewis' field on my way to Carmen's. She was 17, gorgeous, well-developed and the worst strip poker player in Asheville. She always lost. Of course, she didn't know how to play poker and I always cheated. It was a hot summer day and I figured she could be naked in three to six hands, depending on whether, or not she had on a bra or shoes. Anyway, I was taking a short cut when Mr. Lewis spotted me. He yelled at me to stop, or he'd shoot. I looked back and saw him aiming a shotgun. I froze. He walked quickly toward me, but at thirty yards traded the shotgun for an axe and then began to run at me. I shifted into God Almighty! gear and sprinted as fast as my teenage legs could. He was no match, but the field ended at a tall stone wall, fifteen feet straight up. I made it to the top just as he arrived at the bottom swinging the axe and promising to cut my head off if he ever saw me again. I zoomed away and avoided his field the rest of the summer.

I skipped Carmen's house that day. I was too sweaty and trembly. Plus, all my testosterone was spent.

Questions

"Daddy? Are you there?"

"Yes, son."

The room was dark and I had been quietly rocking after reciting a bedtime story. I thought he was asleep.

"Right now it's dark, but why is it ever light?"

"Well. God said, "Let there be light."

"Yeah. I know, but what did Einstein say?"

"Oh boy, I'm not sure. We'll have to look that up tomorrow. Now it's time to go to sleep."

He paused a few moments.

"'Cause I know about the earth spinning around and day and night and all, but I was just wondering about what light actually is."

"Can we sleep on it?"

"Okay daddy, but I have just one more question…"

"What's that, son?"

"How come when we're supposed to love everybody are there so many mean people?"

"Now that's another good one, son. We'll talk about that tomorrow. Close your eyes and turn off your brain for tonight. I'll see ya in the morning. Okay?"

He let out an exasperated sigh and rolled over, facing away from me. I continued to rock back and forth and ponder his precocious queries. I had to smile, this insightful five-year old could give me a run for my money.

He's very smart. We had him tested. My mother administered the test and declared him three times smarter than I could ever be. I believe her 'cause she's twice as smart as I ever was. And I'm no dummy. I've been to college and around the world. I've seen a lot of things and have read a thousand books. I even watch *Jeopardy* and get a few answers right. But this little guy is shrewd and challenges me to explore myself and the workings of the universe.

Yesterday he asked why people need to sleep. I answered, "I'm not exactly sure. I think that our brains get tired, too many chemicals build up. We have to let our thoughts rest and the chemicals dissolve."

"Well that artist guy didn't."

"What artist guy? Michelangelo, or da Vinci?

"No. Piloso."

"You mean Picasso?"

"Yeah, Picasso. He never had to sleep."

"Where'd ya hear that?"

"At school today."

"You mean you guys talk about Picasso in kindergarten?"

"Yep. He just painted and painted and only rested some sittin' straight up in a wooden chair.

I had to laugh and said, "Maybe that's why his paintings are so weird."

That evening we looked at a bunch of Picasso's works on line and tried to guess what he was thinking when he painted them. My son's answers were a combination of laughable childish conjectures and avant-garde genius. He amazed me.

A few days ago, after we'd been shopping in a crowded mall, he asked, "Daddy, do you ever get lonely?"

I answered, "Well, sometimes a little. My body may be alone, but in my heart I always have you and mommy with me. So, I'm never really all alone."

"That's what I do, too. I think about you and mommy all the time and how much I love you."

My eyes welled and my spine tingled as I thought of my little boy and the love of my life. I wanted to hug him tight and force him to feel all the love I have for him, all the hopes and dreams I have for us.

I fell asleep in the rocking chair and dreamed about the three of us on Christmas morning. I could smell the pine tree and the cookie-dough candles. His little eyes were as wide as could be and filled with excitement as he raced from one gift to the next shaking the packages and guessing their contents.

I awakened as he crawled into my lap and folded his arms around my neck.

"Hey, what're you doing? You're supposed to be asleep."

"I was, but then I woke up and was a little bit lonely."

I held him close and pushed the rocker to and fro. I hummed a tune that my mother used to sing to me as she rocked me to sleep. I closed my eyes, but in a few minutes he whispered, "Daddy, who will answer all my questions after you go to heaven to be with mommy?"

My heart skipped a beat and my head filled with pressure. My eyes began to flood.

"You will … and you'll tell them to your own son."

Silence then, a couple of sniffles as he fought tears. I waited, my heart pounding. Shortly, his body jerked, then relaxed. Soon, I heard him snore softly; his little brain finally at rest. I slept in the rocker all that night, my son tight against my chest, our hearts an inch apart, almost one.

Mountain Bike Murders – Part 1

A freshly cut sapling, strong as a steel rod, was jammed into the bike's front wheel. It stopped spinning immediately, but the rider did not. The rear of the mountain bike and its owner began a somersault that ended when the biker crashed face-first into the rocks. Then the machine slammed down on the back of his neck. One pedal didn't release properly and his ankle snapped. He lay dazed in the dirt in terrible pain with two jagged teeth and the taste of blood. He spat red. There was a big gash in his elbow. The broken leg bent at an odd angle and tortured him with nauseating shocks. The wind had been knocked out of him, he could hardly breathe. As he rolled over to unclip the busted leg from the bike, a new pain tore through his chest. *A broken rib?* No, the intense agony repeated itself again and again, pounding and sharp, in his chest, in his gut, in his neck. *Can't breathe. Can't breathe!*

Crimson stained the path where he hit the rocks. A bloody trail proved he crawled ten feet where he died trying to escape his attacker. He was found by a hiker on a trail two and a half miles from the road in Pisgah National Forest.

Three weeks later, two bikers discovered another body on a mountain trail. Sheriff's Deputies were guided to the site in DuPont State Forest to find David Forst, a 36-year old bartender, crumpled in a rhododendron with multiple stab wounds. A length of thin nylon rope was strung across the trail and it looked like Mr. Forst had been "clotheslined" by it. A deep horizontal gash appeared across his neck, maybe fracturing his trachea and definitely knocking him off his bike.

An autopsy confirmed an injured windpipe and described thirteen separate knife wounds. Most were deep wounds to the chest and neck, but several were found on the victim's hands and arms, evidence of self defense.

Two brutal murders, no clues and no obvious motive; the biking community held its breath, the police marked time, impotent.

A month later a third body was found, this time in Bent Creek Experimental Forest, only minutes from Asheville. The victim was another robust male mountain biker. His mutilated body was discovered by a cross-country running team, eight adolescents and their coach. Investigators were a bit miffed by the many sneaker prints corrupting the crime scene and by two puddles of bile and Power Bar slurry, but they understood.

This time, the corpse was lying face up. There was no blood trail. Large quantities of blood had flooded his clothing and bubbled out his mouth. The pool spread onto the autumn leaves and had soaked into the dirt; some had coagulated to become a rubbery puddle the flies feasted on. Unlike the other two victims, this one's eyes had been cut out. They lay beside his head lacerated and sightless.

Jason Spencer had been on a birthday ride, according to his family. He rode for his daughter who could not. She turned eleven that day. She couldn't ride because of cerebral palsy. Her hero rode for her and planned to play the helmet cam footage during her party that evening.

The Bent Creek murder site was different from the first two in other ways. First, there were no signs of attack prior to the murder: no sticks in the spokes, no rope across the trail. Spencer's helmet, minus the video camera, hung from a handlebar and his bike stood propped against a nearby tree. Second, the biker had been stabbed only four times in his torso: one was a direct hit in the heart, two deeply punctured Spencer's right lung and the other sliced into his neck, his esophagus and blood vessels torn to pieces. Also, this victim's groin had been knifed repeatedly. Most important, cops found a bloody hunting knife.

The Blue Ridge Mountains had a serial killer; the knife had fingerprints. They were submitted to the FBI's database. Their super-powerful computer compares all known fingerprints and can find a match in less than two hours. The prints on the bloody hunting knife matched some archived in Virginia. The print's owner had a Greenville, South Carolina address.

At 3:30 in the morning, two days after finding the mutilated corpse in Bent Creek, a SWAT team surrounds a country home off the Greenville Highway. Cops crash through the door. With handcuffs, they capture the villain; they also discover the first victim.

Mountain Bike Murders – Part 2

The best time to get away with a crime is after dark, but sometimes you need a little light to pull it off.

"Thanks so much for helping me out."

"No problem. I'd hate to see ya stuck out here in the dark trying to fix this tire."

She moved fast, like a sparrow snatching ants from hot pavement. He was proud to help a lady in distress and she was gorgeous – athletic and well-endowed. As he reconnected the wheel to the bike, she darted around collecting her tools, water pack and helmet. He smiled at her form.

"Just about done. Let me tighten this down…"

The flash in the corner of his eye was lightning fast, the agony in his chest was immediate. His mind reeled with questions as he crumpled to the ground. Blood bubbled from his mouth and the chest wound sucked air with each breath. *What happened?* He lost consciousness.

"Moron," she said, but he couldn't hear.

In these deep woods, dark falls quickly and now it was almost black. She spit on him and flipped her bike over, ready to ride. But before she could race away, there were lights rounding the bend. Two riders would be there in a seconds. No time to escape. No time to hide the body. Think.

She yanked off her shirt, covered his bloody chest with it and mounted him. Two brilliant lights illuminated the trail and the bare-breasted woman riding her man. The bikers shot past, embarrassed.

Crap! Crap! Crap!

She redressed and at top speed pedaled away in the opposite direction. She almost puked. *What a close call.*

With her bike thrown into the SUV, she drove back to Greenville. It was only 40 minutes from the crime, but far enough to reduce suspicions. This was her third murder and she planned it to be her last. The killings could not erase her pain, but they helped.

On the way down the mountain old memories replayed in her mind – a beautiful autumn day, crisp and breezy, oranges and yellows coloring the forest and a brand new bike, full carbon, top of the line, a racing machine. She felt like a superhero, rocketing around the trails and blasting through clear, cold creeks. She was smiling as she zoomed through the curve and then, lights out. They hit head on. When she regained consciousness, her face was bleeding and her head ached like never before. Her shorts were off, she felt sore and full. She had been raped.

She had gotten counseling; the words sounded nice, the sympathy seemed sincere. It helped a little, but she wanted revenge. For months she had been frequenting the bike trails and the parking lots, searching for him. She wrung out her brain trying to remember his face, that split second before the crash. Nothing. Life had been hopeless since that day. She would never find him. She found a different plan. It wouldn't even the score, nothing ever would, but at least it was something. She would be the victor instead of the victim.

At home, she burned her bloody bike shirt in the fireplace and threw in the sports bra and cycling pants for good measure. Next, she washed off the bike to remove any of his fingerprints. Then, she emptied the hydration pack to wipe down the tools.

CRAP!! Oh my God!! Where the hell is the knife!?

Bile shot into the back of her mouth and exploded onto the carpet. Her heart pounded, her head filled with pressure and dread. She almost fainted. The knife was at the scene and there was nothing she could do about it.

Crap! Crap! Crap! What to do? What to do? Mexico? Get lost in a big city. New York, L.A.? Take a deep breath, calm down. There's nothing to tie that knife to me and nothing else from the other two. Everything happened in Asheville, I'm in Greenville. It's okay. It'll be all right. Don't freak out. It'll be all right.

His body was discovered the next morning. Like the other two, there were no immediate suspects, but this time the murder weapon was found beside the body and there were fingerprints on the bloody knife.

The prints matched some filed in Newport News twenty years ago. Then, a seventeen year old girl, Beth Pressley had attended a sorority party and was arrested for underage drinking. She had forgotten all about that. Now, the woman was a top athlete in the area. She raced mountain bikes and ruled the triathlon circuit. She was beautiful, single, and owned a bike shop.

Asheville's Detective Becky Ross remembered Ms. Pressley when the name on the fingerprints was cross-referenced with department files. Ross had handled the case. Beth had been raped in Bent Creek two years ago, and no culprit was ever found. She called the Greenville police.

For two years, Beth Pressley could barely catch her breath. The rapist had stolen her dignity and self-worth. She was angry and depressed. She felt dead. She dreamed only of revenge. For two years, Beth had been held prisoner by fear and distrust. Sadly, vengeance will steal the remainder of her years. She got life without parole.

Five Minute Mystery

Richard Strupp had the world by the tail: a big money job, a million dollar home, expensive cars, and a trophy wife. He pampered himself with the best that life offers: designer clothes, gourmet meals and world class vacations. He also had two young girlfriends and regularly hired prostitutes.

He was clever. He had everything timed and managed his life to keep everyone clueless of his affairs.

He was found shot to death in his car.

Rachel Strupp was clever also. She had noticed little details, became suspicious and checked into things. One thing she found was a mini-spycam in his car.

She cried when the cops phoned her and reported Richard's murder.

Strupp was discovered slumped against the driver's door with three bullet wounds in his chest, all from point-blank range. Three 9mm shell casings lay on the floor. They also found the spy camera mounted on the rearview mirror. The memory card showed him being intimate with women other than his wife. The most recent, according to the time stamp, was an Asian woman with thick black hair.

Strupp and his Range Rover were found in a strip mall parking lot. Video surveillance showed the car pulling in at 8:52 A.M. and within seconds a dark-haired woman fleeing. Four blocks away, at 8:46, the same dark-haired woman showed up. She stood on the corner and seemed to be waiting on someone. Her skirt was shamefully short. Large dark glasses and elbow-length gloves made her look like a hooker. The traffic video showed cars slowing as drivers checked her out. At 8:49, she raised her top, exposing her breasts. Traffic almost stopped. Richard Strupp had to stop. The woman rushed to the passenger door, yanked it open and jumped inside. After 21 seconds, the Rover began again, rounded the corner and disappeared from view.

Detectives interrogated everyone, just like on television. Most everyone had an airtight alibi, except Lucy Chew, a well known prostitute with a fiery temper.

Two hours after being interrogated, Ms. Chew was onboard a flight headed to Hong Kong. She was taking no chances. The cops had played the recording of Lucy and Strupp having sex and an argument about payment. She slapped him hard. He slapped her back. She was the lead suspect. She was never seen again.

Ten years later, Rachel's guts still twisted when she thought about that day. The cops grilled Rachel. Where was she at the time of the murder? Could she prove it? Did she know about the affairs? Did she have Richard murdered? Was she cheating on him? How much was his life insurance worth? What would she do with all the money? And on and on.

She told them she'd been at a body sculpting class, then jogged six miles. Her Garmin GPS exercise monitor would show the times and the route. It took an hour and was in the opposite direction from where Richard was found. And she'd made two calls during that time. Her position could be confirmed through cell tower triangulation.

What she didn't tell police was that she had found the mini-cam, watched the recordings, and executed the perfect murder.

Rachel was clever. She had timed everything, her plan was foolproof. Richard left the house at exactly 8:40. He was always at the intersection of Commerce and Independence at 8:50. He turned right and arrived at his office at 9:00. She attended the 7:30 class to have witnesses. At 8:30 she was ready to run. She told her friend that she wanted to run some hills and she'd meet her at the park. Secretly, she tucked the GPS unit into Becky's baby jogger. At 8:35 Becky began to run. Rachel sprinted to the back of the building and hopped on her bike. She raced to the strip mall lot in less than five minutes and dumped the bike out of any camera's view. She pulled on a mini skirt, glasses, wig and gloves as she pushed through thick bushes and arrived at the crossroads at 8:46, then waited till she saw Richard. She created a stir by pulling up her shirt. Cars slowed and stopped. She jumped in the Range Rover, shot Richard and then threw her left leg over the console. She drove from the passenger seat, like some mail carriers do and parked in the strip mall four blocks away. Its camera would show a dark-haired woman fleeing the Rover.

Back in the bushes, she stuffed the disguise into her small pack, grabbed the bike and pedaled to the park, arriving two minutes ahead of her friend. At the water fountain they each took a few sips. Rachel tickled the baby and slyly retrieved the GPS unit. She completed the run and made two cell calls. The time stamps on the GPS coordinates and cell phone signals proved where she was and when.

She got off scot-free.

The Note

I got out of work early today, 10 o'clock – and what a perfect day. I sped home, downed a Gatorade, loaded my bike, and zoomed to the trails. Boy, was I excited.

As I eased into my favorite secluded parking spot, I saw Frank's white Chevy van and my wife's Volvo. Becky's been training a lot lately, getting ready for a half Ironman, but I thought she was at work today.

I walked over to her car – her bike still in the back and Frank's propped against the van. It seemed odd. I figured they must be trail running – be back soon for the bikes.

As I stepped away, I heard a muffled voice from inside the van and Becky's distinctive giggle. My spine tingled. The van doesn't have side or back windows, so I couldn't see in without going around front. That's exactly what I did. I quietly eased around the van, staying out of the rearview mirror's reflection. They weren't in the front seats. They were in the back and I'd seen in there before; it was loaded with recreation equipment and a mattress. I stood silently beside the passenger door with its window partially opened and listened.

I heard two soft voices teasing with intermittent notes of surprise and satisfied laughter. The van began to rock gently. My face flashed crimson, my guts twisted.

Becky's cheating on me, she's screwing Frank.

I should've seen it coming, he's a handsome young lawyer and she's a beautiful athletic woman. They've known each other for several years and sometimes train together.

I lost it. My brain exploded with anger.

I crept back to the truck and got my pistol. My whole body shook, my hands so badly I could barely hold the gun. *This is wrong, this is all wrong,* I told myself.

I couldn't help it, rage forced me to chamber a round, ease the truck door shut and tiptoe back to the van. I resumed my position near the passenger door and listened. The murmur of intimacy wafted out the window. My blood boiled, my knees turned to jelly, but I forced my legs to move round to the rear of the van.

I stood for a minute with my left hand choking the door's handle and my right crushing the gun. Should I yank the door open and blast them to pieces, or give 'em a chance to explain, then kill 'em both? Maybe I should just shoot Becky, after all Frank's a typical man and what normal, red-blooded American male could resist my gorgeous wife. She's cheating on me, but he can't help himself. I lowered the pistol for a moment and took some deep breaths. I was goin' nuts. I was about to kill my wife.

This is crazy – absolutely insane.

Maybe I should just kill myself. We've been arguing a lot lately – guess she's found a better friend.

I should kill myself and not have to worry about this.

My heart was pounding out of my chest and I was breathing like I'd run a triathlon. Sweat fell off my forehead, tears filled my eyes. I'd never been angrier, or more frightened. I told myself, this is it – the last straw. Forget a divorce. I'd lose everything anyway.

The van rocked harder. At first there was silence, then rhythmic groans and oaths and pleas for more.

"Don't stop! Don't stop!" I heard my wife beg.

Grunting from him.

I went berserk, snatched the rear door open and shoved the gun through the gap. Sure enough, they were in the middle of it, going to town in a position that I'd never enjoyed with my wife. Fury electrified me. I pulled the trigger and blew out the windshield. They twisted when the door opened, uncoupled, and curled into balls with the gun shot. She started wailing, sobbing uncontrollably.

Panic replaced ecstasy. Words flooded the van. He tried to explain, she to apologize, and each appealed to reason. Naked and ashamed they begged for mercy.

I shot them both three times – killed them dead.

I write this so you'll know exactly what went down. I'm aware it's a bit long-winded. Maybe I should've simply said I caught 'em together and killed 'em, or maybe I shouldn't have said anything at all. But I've had five hours to think and plan and write. My mom has picked up the kids from school and they're at piano lessons about now. They'll be done around 6:30.

I heard the dog bark when you all drove up and I hear you knocking on the door right now. I'm not going to open up. I know you're the police and I'm going to make you earn your money. I will tell ya this is the same gun that killed Becky and Frank, so you can save some cash on the ballistics test. And yes, I went nuts. Sane people don't murder.

I hear ya – you're gonna bust down the door. Come on, I'm ready for you – saved one bullet. I hate to put you all through this and I pray my kids will someday forgive me, but I'm not wearing your handcuffs and I'm not spending the rest of my life in prison.

Bang!

Rain

I love rain, probably inherited it from my mother. She grew up in the Deep South where rain, within reason, meant money. Her father and his father were poor, uneducated, dirt farmers whose fortunes were directly tied to the weather. Rain was their lifeblood.

In fact, I view rain as the lifeblood of the Earth: crucial, non-negotiable. Without rain our planet would simply be a chunk of rock spinning through infinity, lifeless as Mars, without appreciation, without us.

Now, don't get me wrong. I love a sunny day. Sunshine is like a mother's love, warm and nurturing. The Sun is essential for life as well; without it our solar system wouldn't exist, our orbiting stone wouldn't circle, and whatever there might be would be frozen and blind. But as mighty as the Sun is, life as we know it requires water, and not only in pools vast or small. We need it to drop from the sky, dispersed throughout the lands.

This morning I sat on the porch before dawn listening to the rain. The system marched up from the Gulf, the rain warm, steady and gentle. I could almost taste salt as the oak leaves danced with the breeze and mist crept across the yard. Moisture caressed my skin, a vaporous cleansing by Mother Earth's love.

As dawn broke, I watched sparrows dodge the drops, flitting here and there across the neighborhood, alighting under parasols of leaves momentarily before darting off to some other refuge. Their antics seemed playful.

I thought about my mother romping about as a child in the Alabama rain, bare-footed, slippery clay between her toes, grinning at the sky, merrily singing childish tunes, the warm drops dotting her face and trickling down her neck as she spun round like Maria in the opening scene from *Sound of Music*.

And I remembered her father at the supper table telling stories about his crops and back-breaking toil. So often the rains were cruel and either washed away his dreams or refused to fall. He died of a heatstroke in a scorched bean field that hadn't seen moisture for a month.

The sun rode higher, vision improved, and the shapeless gray gauze that blanketed the horizon began to take form. The rain ceased, the cloudbank cracked apart, and Sol's rays fell through the gaps. One beam raced across the neighborhood and briefly sojourned directly overhead as the clouds churned in the breeze. The image snatched my favorite memory from twenty years ago and replayed it in my mind.

I had met Kelly only days before and now we sat on a Pompano beach, on a blanket facing the waves, holding hands, searching each other's eyes for signs of a future together. She was (and still is) a raven-haired beauty with a Hollywood smile and infectious laugh. Her slender fingers were laced into mine and occasionally gripped tighter as she made some point, or wished to convey romantic interest. We spoke of our dreams and hopes for the future. We sat on the doorstep of true love.

The day was incredible. Warm sun caressed us as clouds slipped by rarely casting us in shadow. Beach-goers sat, or swam, or combed the sands in search of anything interesting. Folks played Frisbee, flew kites, and chased errant children through shallow waves. We simply sat entranced with each other. I'll never forget how my heart pounded when she agreed to our first date and how it felt to sit beside her on that beach: a miracle.

In the early afternoon, the southern horizon grew dark, lightning flashed not a mile away. A thick gray curtain of rain fell from an ominous dark cloud and most of the beach-folk packed up and left. We stayed put, taking our chances, not wanting our bliss to end. The rain and thunder advanced up the beach and soon began to rinse the salt water off our bodies. Warm, fat drops showered us and we laughed. I put my arm around her, we leaned together and watched sunbeams cut through the cloud to light the ocean in patches of blue and emerald and white frothy waves.

The gentle rain turned mean for a few minutes, then drizzled and retreated. The storm cloud raced toward Africa, the sun returned to dry us. Still we sat, now on a soaked blanket and now alone. We had survived our first storm and it seemed a good omen. As if on cue our lips met, our first kiss. It lasted forever and wasn't long enough.

That memory melted into another favorite rain-related recollection.

In late spring, Kelly and I moved to Alaska where we shared more rain showers, kisses, thrills, tribulations, and an apartment. The thrills and tribulations became part of our adventures together that have welded us to one another. We became best friends: inseparable and our destinies one. Those adventures will have to be told some other time.

After Alaska, we moved around the country: the mountains of Tennessee, Colorado, Arizona, Montana, and finally North Carolina, where I grew up. Because of jobs we sometimes had to live apart, but we were always faithful and true to each other.

My favorite memory took place on the rocky spine of the high altitude grassy bald, Black Balsam Knob. We had hiked the Art Loeb trail to its pinnacle where a brass plaque declares the mountain's name and altitude, 6,214ft. The morning had been perfect and we picnicked near the plaque. As often happens on this prominence, a rain squall blew in from the west. The light, cool rain refreshed us and we laughed about the many times we'd gotten wet during our courtship. It wasn't long before the rains gave way to blue skies, summer sun, and the most brilliant double rainbow I'd ever seen. Another omen. We were holding hands tightly and remarking at our good fortune when Kelly turned to me, took my other hand in hers and said, "Let's get married."

First and Last

The first dead guy I ever saw had most of his head blown off. I was 15 years old and a volunteer in the emergency room on weekends. I don't remember the guy's name, but I do remember he had come from Madison County. I guess he lost the gun battle. A shotgun blast had entered his right eye and torn off most of that side of his head. Some bloody gelatinous brain tissue remained in the cavity, some had oozed onto the gurney sheets, most had clotted in his nappy shoulder length hair. His nose, mouth and right cheek were distorted and blackened from powder burns. The sight was awful, the smell was worse: blood, tobacco and whiskey. I nearly puked. I helped take him to the morgue and place him on the cold stainless steel autopsy table.

That was over forty years ago and I've seen scores of dead folks since. Some have come in dead, most have needed help but were unsalvageable, and there've been a few that I've helped to die.

The second person I saw dead had suffered a heart attack and lay intact and peaceful in his hospital bed. I helped take him to the morgue, put him in a long freezer drawer, and slide it shut. I had nightmares about him. What if he wasn't dead? The first guy was obviously gone, but the second guy could have been faking.

I was still 15 when I witnessed one of the most heart-wrenching deaths I can recall.

I had loaded a distressed pregnant lady into a wheelchair and rushed her into the ER. I told the nurse that the miscarriage tissue was still in the back seat of the woman's car. She sent me to collect it. I scooped the placenta and tiny baby into a plastic tub. The child was translucent and its heart was beating. I rushed in and showed it to the charge nurse. There was nothing anyone could do. We watched it die.

Another unforgettable death I witnessed was a 36-year old man. He had AIDS. I was his nurse. He was in an isolation room. I had to wear a gown, gloves and mask. He sensed the end was near and had no friends or family on hand. The stigma of AIDS had chased them off. I saw terror in his eyes. He was about to die alone, a pariah. He was pitiful.

He gasped and struggled to say, "Will you stay with me?"

I took off my gloves and held his hand. The corners of his mouth turned up. His grip faded, his eyes shut. In a moment, he took his final raspy breath, his pulse weakened. I flushed and challenged the lump in my throat. I leaned into his ear and said, "It's okay," and called his name, "You can have peace now. Rest easy and find peace."

Now, this story is about death, but I've saved many lives. I'll tell you about one.

Bobby was 41, mentally challenged, and in the ICU because of a lethal heart rhythm. Sometimes his heart would race so fast it couldn't pump blood effectively, ventricular tachycardia. While I helped him bathe, his heart rate skyrocketed. As he lost consciousness, I drilled his left chest with my fist: a precordial thump. It's like a reset switch. His heart rate slowed and became regular. He awakened.

"Bobby, are you OK?"

"Yeah, Mike. I guess so, …but Mike?… why'd ya hit me?"

As of this writing, the last person I've seen dead involves a tragic tale with far-reaching consequences. I met the deceased at 2:30 A.M. She was an organ donor. I administered anesthesia. You might ask why a dead person would need my services and it's a great question. She was brain dead; the essence of this mother of three was gone, never to return, yet her other bodily functions remained viable – for a short while. The general public probably doesn't ponder how organ donation and transplant processes work. They just accept that someone has died and gifted their organs to improve someone else's quality of life. My role is to keep all systems functioning optimally with oxygen, fluids, and drugs.

The back story for this tale began four days before we met. Amy (not her real name) and her family and friends were celebrating her daughter's sixth birthday with a cookout in their backyard. They were having a wonderful time playing games, opening presents, and eating hotdogs. When the birthday girl opened her final present, the incredible one from her grandmother, Amy gasped in excitement and drew in a huge breath. Her mouth was full of food. The hotdog was pulled into her windpipe so forcefully that she couldn't cough it out.

In fact, she couldn't breathe around the partially chewed wad. Amy choked. She tried to cough, but she gagged and panicked. Others tried to help. They used the Heimlich maneuver repeatedly, but to no avail.

Amy's face turned red, then purple, then blue. She collapsed. 911 arrived within minutes, but the damage was done. Amy's brain had been without oxygen for too long and it was dead. CPR kept blood flowing to her other organs and the wad of meat was eventually extracted by the paramedics, allowing some air in.

She was whisked to the hospital and placed on life support. Every effort was made to revive her brain, but the doctors failed. She was declared brain dead two days after the birthday party.

At 2:48 A.M., we all stood silently and listened to the transplant coordinator read aloud a heartfelt thanks form the scheduled recipients of Amy's precious gifts and society's thanks to Amy and her family.

At 2:51 the operation began. Within hours, an eight-year old in Cleveland and a school teacher from Des Moines would each receive a new kidney, a Methodist minister dying from liver cancer would get a new chance at life, and a young mother in California, wracked by diabetes her whole life, would receive a new pancreas.

Amy's tragic death devastated the lives of those close to her, but incalculably improved the lives of strangers who will never forget Amy's precious, selfless gifts.

Flying Crocodiles

BaBang! Thud! Brrizzppp!

It was 3am. The hollow plastic explosion startled us all. Kelly bolted upright, "What the…?" She dug her fingernails into my face. I jumped up with an oath and fists at the ready.

Kylie began to wail, "Oh no! Mommy, no, no! Don't let 'em get me! Please! Please!"

Kelly flew to her baby's side. I checked the shower stall. Sure enough the suction-cupped soap container had jumped from the wall and lay sprawled in the tub minus its contents. I cussed it and checked the rest of the house for burglars.

I heard Kelly say, "No one's gonna get you baby, it was just something falling in the shower. No one's gonna hurt you."

"Yes, they are, mommy. They're trying to get in. I heard them."

"It's nothing, sweetheart, only the soap dish in the shower. That's all."

"No, it's not! I heard them outside my window and one crashed into the wall."

"Kylie, you were dreaming. The noise was the soap dish…"

"No, mommy, I saw them too."

"Baby, it was just a dream. What'd ya think you saw?"

"Crocodiles!"

"What? Crocodiles? That was just a dream. I'll hold you till ya go back to sleep."

"No, mommy, they're real. They're outside my window."

"Baby, there aren't any crocodiles around here. Plus all the doors are locked. They couldn't get in if they wanted to."

"They have wings. They can fly. They were trying to come in my window, but smacked the side of the house."

"No burglars," I reported as I walked into Kylie's bedroom.

Her mother held her close, but she was still crying.

"What's wrong, sweetheart?" I asked.

"She's afraid of flying crocodiles."

"Baby, there's no such thing."

"Yes, there is. Papa told me a story about 'em. They can fly and shoot flames out their mouths. Sometimes they eat little children if they misbehave."

Kelly and I both chimed in, "No, honey. They aren't real. Papa must've told you a fairy tale."

"No, he didn't. He said it was a true story his grandmother told him and he's seen 'em too – in Savannah were he grew up. And they ate his neighbor who was a bully and didn't listen to his mommy."

Kelly hugged tighter and said, "Kylie, I promise there's no such thing as a flying crocodile."

I said, "No, there's not and I'll have Papa tell ya that next time he baby-sits you, okay? Now, let's go back to sleep. We've got a big day tomorrow."

"Can I sleep in your bed?"

Reluctantly we both said, "Okay."

She flipped and twisted and squirmed until exhaustion doused all her fires. She came to rest with her elbow in my face, then feet in my back once I turned away.

We were worn out and irritable when we arrived in Florida. For months we'd made plans to visit Walt Disney World and Busch Gardens. Kylie was quite excited to see Mickey and Minnie, princesses and elephants. She couldn't wait to ride roller coasters and eat cotton candy, but her excitement faltered as the plane neared Orlando. Videos advertised area attractions, including alligators. Her eyes got big and she wrung Kelly's hand. Fear turned to dread as we neared the park. Billboards showed giant alligators, and ringing the parking lot were a dozen huge helium balloons. One was an alligator. She thought it was a flying crocodile and refused to get out of the car. She made a scene. The squabble bordered on combat, so much so that a security guard intervened. He listened and kindly explained that the balloon was an alligator, the real ones were confined and of no danger. Kylie was intransigent; there was no way she was going into the park. She pitched a fit. We never saw Busch Gardens. Disney was better. Kelly scouted it out while Kylie and I played cards in the hotel room. We avoided anything reptilian in the park.

All of that was a long time ago. Now I'm the grandfather baby-sitting Kylie's child. Yesterday at naptime she said, "Granpa, will you tell me a story?"

So I began one my father had told me – the one about a black stallion and a puppy.

"No not that one, Granpa. Tell one about a flying crocodile."

My neck hairs sprang to attention. “What? There’s no such thing as flying crocodiles.”

“Uh huh, yes there are, and they’re magic too! Mommy told me all about ‘em.”

“She did?” The memories of that awful night and vacation came flooding back.

“Uh huh, they can fly and they protect little children. They help kids learn to read and even know if there’s any candy hidden in the pantry!”

Games

Ya seen the news lately?

Yeah, what?

All these lunatics setting fires in California and kidnapping the senator's daughter and that survivalist in Pennsylvania cappin' those cops?

Yeah, they're makin' quite a name for themselves. Prob'ly go down in the history books. We oughta do something crazy.

Like what? Sneak in the grade school and blow some little kids away? Or take out some wrinkled old blue hairs walkin' around the mall?

Naw, that's too easy. Only punks would do it that way. It'd be like goin' to the pound and shootin' dogs in their cages. Where's the sport in that?

Yeah, I guess you're right. Well, what then?

We need to make it more challenging, a deadly game. Let 'em know we're after 'em so's they've got guns and we've got to outsmart 'em.

Like call out some motorcycle gang, or the cops, or the Navy Seals?

God, no, not the Seals, they'll murder us for sure, but something like that.

Hey, what about some of those ISIS guys? Everybody hates terrorists. We could bitch slap 'em on Facebook, or something, insult Islam, or Mohammad, set up a meet where we blast 'em with machine guns and pipe bombs. Blow 'em all to pieces and become heroes!

Not bad, not bad at all. Here's how we'll do it: first we check out the cyber traffic. Ya know, what's on Facebook and YouTube and such. Learn as much about 'em as we can, even pretend to be a sympathizer maybe.

Yeah, they got websites and blogs and all kinds of stuff for recruitment.

Then find a great spot, set up an ambush – like those cowards do in Afghanistan.

We're not cowards.

No, but we gotta figure out how to get 'em here and where to have a battle that's in our favor.

What about the Jewish Community Center, or that synagogue by Weaver Park, its got a great escape route – a huge storm drain you can run through and it goes for about a half mile. Ya pop out by the university. Put a bomb at the end and whoever's chasing us is a goner.

Fantastic! They'll go crazy. They hate Jews almost as much as American infidels.

Okay. Keep your mouth shut, and don't say nothing to nobody. It'll be just the two of us. We've got plenty of firepower. Don't forget let's check the ammo.

I got dibbs on the M–60.

It's too heavy for you. Ya need to be able to run with it.

Then I get an AK and a shotgun and most of the grenades.

They're heavy, too.

I'll carry two or three and stash the rest along our escape route.

That'll probably work. What about that fertilizer and diesel you been braggin about?

I used it all, but I got some new stuff, even more powerful. I'll make us a bunch of bombs and pack em with drywall screws. That'll rip 'em to shreds!

Now you're talking. I'll string some trip wires, connect 'em to your IEDs.

Okay, check this out. Here's the satellite view of that synagogue. The drain runs from about here to here. If we engage in the parking lot, here, we can surprise 'em from these trees and set off the first bombs as they get out of their cars.

How many ya think we can take on, just the two of us?

Well, that depends….maybe a dozen? I'm not sure.

Think we should ask Terry to help us out? He's been wantin' to kill somebody real bad.

Hmmm, maybe, but he's such a big mouth.

Yeah, but he's a crack shot and says he's got a couple of machine guns, a Thompson, and an H&K from Germany that's super bad. We might need him, especially if they bring a bunch of guys.

Let's think about it.

Well, anyway, let's walk over to the synagogue, check it out. And tonight let's check the internet, get on their sites and start pissin' 'em off.

This is gonna be so cool!

Yeah, I hope they bite and I hope the NSA don't swoop in and ruin the plan. They'll be listenin' ya know.

Think we should we use a computer at the library, throw 'em off our trail?

That's a good idea also.

I'm stoked.

Me too, but remember this ain't no video game. You gotta be ready to die. I mean die for real. These guys won't be playing. We kill them, or they kill us.

Yeah, I know… it's for real. Like everything. Yeah, yeah… Hey wait! Can we do it Saturday afternoon, or Sunday?

I guess so, why?

Saturday morning I got Drivers Ed.

Part 2

Part 2, you say? Yes Part 2. I had so much fun telling you all those stories (and yeah, I know there are more than 31) that I couldn't stop writing. So here are some longer tales. Now, I still want you to adhere to the five minute rule in the bathroom, but it's okay to read these in their entirety while parked on the sofa, or in the recliner, etc.

Epiphany Ridge

"Why in the hell do you do these things to yourself, Mike?" I screamed into the wilderness. I'd fallen for the hundredth time, was battered and exhausted. The knee-deep snow and nearly impenetrable ice-coated forest did not reply. It didn't care. I was alone, dehydrated, and a little frightened. Now, I've been in similar situations before: in the Montana wilderness, on Alaskan rivers, the high peaks of Colorado, the parched canyons of Utah, but I'd never felt so isolated, tired, and defeated. This ice-coated prison captured my cries, absorbed my anguish, and remained silent while I struggled to regain my footing, my dignity, and my courage.

The day had begun well enough. Actually, it had begun a couple of weeks before. The winter weather had been brutal that year. Western North Carolina had suffered a string of bitterly cold weeks and more snow and ice accumulation than I'd seen in years. Wild winds, crazy cold, knee-deep snow and tree-busting ice storms demanded that I shoulder a pack, don skis, and traipse into the Shining Rock Wilderness for a solo adventure. I began planning and organizing two weeks beforehand.

Over several days, I gathered together all of my cold weather backpacking gear: a cozy tent, 5-degree sleeping bag, stove and water filter. I assembled clothing options and pared them down to only the essentials plus a second pair of gloves, an extra fleece, and a second hat – a purple "bomber" style Gore-Tex hat worthy of a Himalayan adventure.

I call it my ugly hat; everyone hates it. It's an awful color and too big, but I love it. Rescue helicopters can see it from miles away and it fits over my head with two toboggans already in place. It's saved my life a couple of times. I can easily find it if I drop it and NO ONE would ever steal it.

The day before my big adventure I remembered I'd given my skis to Goodwill and now needed to borrow some. My dad no longer used the ones I gave him twenty-six years ago, so I borrowed his. Once I put them on I realized why I had given mine away. Mine, too, had been just as old and worn out. They were skinny, plastic-edged cross country skis with fish scales on the bottom for traction. Even when they were new, they were difficult to control. And now, with imperceptible fish scales, a forty-five pound backpack and an ice coating on the trail they were truly dangerous – bordering on insane. But that didn't stop me. The disintegrating sloppy ski boots compounded the imprecise steering and added to the adventure – cranked up the difficulty a notch. I could usually go forward and I could turn a little some of the time, but stopping, or even standing still on the crusty, icy snow, was not assured. Ahh, "The Struggle." Adversity builds character!

I parked the truck and was surprised to find a few other hardy souls already playing in the area. This is not an easy place to get to. It's far from any town, miles on steep twisty roads that sometimes don't have guardrails, and on this day, the last few miles were blanketed with snow and ice. Before I could park, I had to convince my 4x4 truck to negotiate a final hundred-yard obstacle course of nearly impenetrable knee-deep snow drifts and frictionless icy ruts. My vehicle spun and bucked and slipped and complained as it has never done before. But after a few tortured minutes of creative coaxing, I parked, shouldered my backpack, clipped into dad's skis, and warily began gliding up the Blue Ridge Parkway.

My footing was unsure, my balance questionable, but my spirits were high. This was going to be a trip to remember. I smiled at myself for being so bold, so ambitious, so determined to meet the forces of Nature, welcome them, work with them – just as I always had.

My smile ended when I spoke aloud to myself, "But don't forget, Mister Smarty Pants, you're fifty-two years old. You ain't superman anymore." And mentally, I listed the most recent evidences of my mortality: a busted shoulder that aggravates me daily and punishes me every night when I should be sleeping; a spine fusion four years ago that tortures me most when I carry a heavy pack; and most recently, a severely sprained ankle that required medical attention, a cam boot, and a six-month rest.

It took a few minutes before I could find a rhythm. Pole, kick, glide? At first it was more like pole, slip, slide, wobble dangerously, and barely recover before gravity forced an undignified crash and an explosion of expletives. As I glided up the Parkway toward Devil's Courthouse, I passed a couple taking photographs of this gorgeous snowy day. They wore heavy coats, hooded and fur-lined. They were short, animated, and used an old school, film-loaded Nikon with a foot-long telescopic lens. They were the quintessential photographers – elderly Japanese mates. I almost laughed out loud as I watched their excited antics, but instead I asked if they would take my picture with my camera. Kindly, they obliged and I kept on trucking.

While I was being photographed another hardy soul (lunatic) on skis skated past and headed in the direction that I was going. He seemed in no hurry so I was able to catch up before long. He was tall and obviously fit. He glided with ease on modern equipment, unlike mine. We exchanged pleasantries and then shared a spirited discussion of where we'd been, what kind of skiing we'd done and learned that we'd both just returned from ice climbing adventures in Colorado. His name was easy to remember: Mike. We skied and chatted for a couple of miles before I left the roadbed to venture onto the Art Loeb Trail.

Here's where the real adventure began.

The Art Loeb Trail is one of my favorite trails. It's thirty miles long and is well used, coursing through deep, moist, silent forests and traversing high altitude, windswept ridgelines on its way from Davidson River Campground near Brevard NC to Camp Daniel Boone located on the Little East Fork of the Pigeon River. The trail crosses the Parkway a couple of miles south of the Black Balsam road and, if you head north at this point, it rapidly ascends a four-hundred foot escarpment littered with roots, rocks, rotting railroad ties, and slippery black dirt. It's a difficult climb in the best of times. The angle, the footing, saw briars, poison ivy, and overgrown rhododendrons seem to conspire and hamper forward progress. The rhododendron's bony-finger branches love to poke eyes and gouge flesh even through heavy clothing. The saw briars attack with wiry strength and razor-sharp, poison-tipped piranha thorns that are mean; they'll chase you. The poison ivy is pervasive from the late spring until autumn frosts cripple it. I'm always on the lookout for it and I give it a wide berth if possible, but it gets me almost every year.

I found the trail marker nearly buried by snow and the trail itself merely an indistinct shallow trough leading into the woods. I stopped, fell, took off the piece of crap worthless skis and donned brand new, sharp, shiny mountaineering crampons. My new buddy just shook his head when I detailed my bold plan: climb this nearly vertical path, ski the ridge, descend through a fantastic copse of mature Balsams, cross the paved road, climb Black Balsam, and set up my camp on the very top. I planned to then carve some big, deep sensuous turns on the balds and high altitude meadows. Mike planned on doing something similar, but not camping overnight. He wished me good luck and continued skiing up the Parkway.

I shouldered my backpack, which now included my skis lashed to its sides using the pockets provided. I had never done this before and I really didn't think of how high these 6-foot long skis would stick into the air. I made my way over to the trailhead and sank into the snow about halfway up to my knee with each step. Oh, no, I thought – post-holing already. This may be harder than I expected. The crampons provided great traction, but my weight was not spread out like when I had the skis on and so I sank and wallowed as I tried to move forward.

I'd struggled up the trail about twenty feet when the towering ski tips caught the branches of some tree. They pulled me backward and almost toppled me, but I held on, squatted down, bent way forward, and bullied my way past. This scene was repeated three or four more times in the next few yards. I was exhausted and hadn't gone 100 feet. Cursing, I took off the pack and removed the offending plastic encumbrances. Now, in each gloved hand, I held a ski and a pole. Carrying them was quite difficult. I couldn't reach all the way around them, they were slippery, and they needed to be held just right to remain balanced and not form an X that would stab the ground in front of me.

While I was rearranging and cussing, I studied the path ahead. It was a horrible tangle of bent vegetation and tree branches all thickly ice-coated and frozen to each other and to the ground. My route was totally blocked about 30 feet ahead. When I got there, I shook the imprisoned branches, but they were iced together as though super-glued. After a minute, I realized that I needed "THE SAW."

For about ten years I have been using an 18-inch pruning saw instead of one of those wimpy 7-inch folding backpacking saws. I get a new one every couple of years so it's razor sharp. These bad boys will zip through a 12-inch oak in about three minutes. Ice is no match.

I cut my way through about ten feet of drooping branches and limbs – yes, and a couple of hateful saw briars. I laughed at the bushes, "You can't stop me. I've got the saw!" And I plodded forward another few feet before I fell, lost both skis and poles and got snow inside my gloves. This was just the beginning of what became a tiring pattern that required a Herculean effort.

The long skinny skis displaced my weight well enough on the Parkway, but in the forest with Ginsu Knife sharp crampons, my feet cut through the crust and plunged deep with every step. The tough crust would fracture just as I placed most of my weight on that foot. It would explode and I'd pitch forward, sink deep and bruise my shins on the exposed icy edge. Again and again this happened. When I got home, I found that my lower legs looked as though they had been beaten with a baseball bat. Every step forward required that I first step up, out of the deep hole that I'd just created, and onto the icy crust. And every step up terminated in forming the next posthole that I had to rescue myself from.

My progress was maddeningly slow. I fell so many times that my shins screamed in pain, my knuckles were bruised, and my hands were wringing wet inside my gloves. My fingers grew stiff and very cold. I dropped the skis and poles a thousand times and they pinched my hands when I fell on them. My forty-five pound backpack kept me off balance and pulled me backwards many times. A forward step up, a plunging "step?" down, an awkward top-heavy wobble sideways, forward, or backwards, and the inevitable topple into deep snow. And every few feet I had to take off the pack, whip out the saw, and cut through the limbs and trees and bushes and branches and briars that were coated with an inch of ice. I had never seen anything like it: an icy prison all around me.

I hadn't been on this particular part of the Art Loeb in about five years, but my memory and the map suggested that I could remove the crampons and return to skiing. How wonderful, I thought. No more postholing. I'll just shush through those trees, glide over to Black Balsam, set up camp and have the best little ole time. But it didn't happen like that.

I did shush for a couple of minutes, but it wasn't easy or fun. I was even more off balance than when I was on the Parkway. The ridge rose and fell. The path twisted and turned. And, of course, within minutes I was once again surrounded by my icy captors. The rhododendron, laurel, wild cherry, and Balsam pines grow tall and strong on the sun-soaked ridge. So do the blueberry, blackberry and other bushes, but now the flora that normally stood six, or ten, or sixteen feet high was bent over acutely, forming arches weighted down by tons of ice. The branches were fused together, their tips buried by two feet of snow. Many times the frozen tendrils were just too numerous, too thick, so I chose a path around the obstacle. And many times it seemed simpler to remove the skis and slide on my belly underneath my icy nemesis.

In some places, the forest was essentially closed to foot travel. Icy tentacles trapped everything except light, and even that was dim. Crawling became my "preferred" mode of travel. Even though it's an inglorious and undignified method of propulsion I have utilized it extensively and honed it to a fine art. Long ago I was awarded the dismal reputation of crawling through thickets whenever backpacking. People from foreign countries know better than to hike with me. At some point I will be crawling. Not because I like being on my hands and knees, but because the only way out of the mess I find myself in requires slithering. Maps have betrayed me; compasses are of no use in Western North Carolina; I don't own a GPS; trail markers are incorrect or non-existent; and following the "well worn trail" only leads you in a circle (right, Dan?). Anyway, I have logged almost as many crawling hours as I have sitting by the campfire hours. And this trip added another 150 minutes to the crawling ledger and zero minutes sitting by the campfire.

So I crawled. And while it may have saved some energy, it still required a tremendous effort.

Zen and the Art of Crawling suggests that we engage in belly travel only when absolutely necessary. It should be our next-to-last option – the last option being quitting. Wriggling along on one's belly is a difficult physical maneuver and the philosophical mindset that must be employed reaches so far into the spiritual realm that even Zen masters sometime require cosmic reinforcement.

The Art suggests paying strict attention while placing your tender hands and knees: avoid sharp rocks and knotted roots and try not to get too muddy. It recommends that you diligently protect your two eyes from being gouged out by hateful branches and concentrate on the nape of your neck. Malevolent arachnids string ambush nets in lower branches and from there dive down shirt collars to inject venom into unprotected tender flesh. Finally, *Crawling Zen* urges us to endure being snagged countless times by fishhook undergrowth. Ignore facial whippings by springy slender branches. Overcome the low hanging forces of Nature that conspire to arrest your progress, cause you to blink and bleed and frustrate you to the point of turning back, abandoning hell on all fours and returning to the bipedal upright world. We must continue forward –no matter what. (Expletives are discouraged, but understood.) Move forward soldier – warrior – hero! Press on. Prevail. Ahhh…The Struggle!

But belly-time on Epiphany Ridge was an all new experience. The sharp rocks and roots were buried and fully padded. The spiders were chillin' out where ever it is they go in the winter. And the bees and snakes and poison ivy were with the spiders.

Winter crawling was different. I didn't have to worry about warm weather issues. But I did have to worry about going blind and I did have to alter my slithering style. From the postholes that I was standing in, I would lean forward with skis and poles in hand, press them down gingerly onto the slick crusty surface and hope they stayed put. Then I angled my belly so that I did not simply plop onto the snow; I tried to glide onto it and use the momentum to help forge ahead. Using my *Zen Crawl*, I inched along. I was still plagued by the inevitable grappling hook limbs snagging the huge pack and stealing my hat. I was further tortured because my battered hands and bruised knees kept plunging through the crusty snow halting hard-earned progress, crippling my determination. Forward meant that I had to dig deep into the crusted snow with all appendages, sinking them. Forward meant filling gloves, socks, and boots full of freezing crystals and powder. It was exhausting. It was frustrating. It seemed endless. But like a good Marine I continued, not too smart, but determined and durable.

Hours passed unnoticed. I became dehydrated, hypoglycemic, and demoralized. But I finally arrived at a known point – a boundary marker for the Parkway. Here the map showed that the trail turned left and followed the ridge down a couple of hundred feet. While consulting the map, I noticed that evening was upon me. I checked my watch and found that I had maybe half an hour before dark. Hurriedly, I turned left and descended through the best openings I could find. Of course, I couldn't use the worn out skis; the slope was too steep, the turns would be too tight. So I postholed and slid on my butt and crawled when necessary. And, you guessed it. I strayed off course.

I later discovered that I should have continued "left" for about two tenths of a mile, then swooped around to the "right" under the towering Balsams that lead to the road. But gravity pulled me through rhodo tunnels and down the hillside more or less in a straight line. I bottomed out (kinda') after dropping a couple of hundred feet. When I stopped to get my bearings, I discovered that I had lost a ski pole – up there, somewhere!

Decisions. Decisions. Going back would be murder. It would take precious minutes that I didn't have. It was now almost dark and I was nowhere near Black Balsam. In fact, I was nowhere near anything! Do I really need that pole? Yes. I can't ski out of this madhouse with only one pole. Hell, I can barely ski with two poles. Crap! I dropped the pack, the skis and the remaining pole, and reluctantly retraced my steps. Did I say that I had descended only two hundred feet? I postholed back to the ridge top. It took forever. I found the stray pole and ran back down the mountainside to where I'd left the pack.

In the failing light, I searched around for any small clearing nearby that was somewhat flat and large enough to fit my tent. Nothing. I shouldered the pack, collected the ski stuff and plodded through the choked forest. Five minutes before pitch black, moonless, wintertime dark, I found the only place almost big enough for my tent. It wasn't flat and it wasn't the right size, but it would have to do. As I erected the tent, I repeatedly postholed into the snow that would be beneath the tent's floor, the snow on which I would sleep.

With only a Therm-A-Rest between me and a dozen knee-deep, frozen footprints, sleep proved to be nearly impossible. I rolled and tumbled and backstroked and cussed my lumpy, bumpy, freezing, crusty, slanted, half-cocked, sliding-off-the-mat, side-hilled, off-route, crappy, hole-in-the-middle, bad shoulder, exhausted, thirsty, too-tired-to-eat, "sleep" spot.

But before I lay awake most of the night, I inflated the sleeping pad and fluffed my sleeping bag and collapsed in it with all of my coats and extra hats and dry gloves on. At first, I buried myself deep in the bag with only my nostrils exposed to the fresh air. I shivered and suffered. I inspected the damage by headlamp light. My fingers were pretty cold, wrinkled, pale, and battered, but they were not in danger of frostbite. My toes worried me more. The front half of both feet were white. I have bad circulation in my doggies and there was a clear demarcation between pink viable flesh and white, sickly, pre-death, wooden, insensate forefoot. I gently massaged them and energetically wiggled my toes for two full hours. And during those two hours I thought about my day – how difficult, how painful, how dangerous.

Why was I off course, in the dead of winter, the worst winter in decades, all alone, exhausted and invisible to search parties? Why did I force myself through the wilderness? Why did I not stay on the Parkway? What if I break a leg or even severely sprain an ankle? Re-sprain the ankle? Boy, if I had to get out of here with my ankle freshly sprained like it was last November, my tough trip through paradise would become an epic, a potentially life-threatening roll of the dice. Why do I push myself to my limits? Why do I need to hold hands with Death? To feel alive? Why do I create adversity - to ensure The Struggle?

After being in the tent for two hours, I was rested enough to attempt to eat. I had brought only twenty ounces of water with me and had drunk half of that during my "trail of tears." I had planned on melting snow into drinking water, but now I was too exhausted to mess with it. I saved the rest of the water for morning and drank the two beers that I had packed in.

Within minutes of finishing the first bottle, circulation returned to my feet. (Alcohol is a great vasodilator.) I noticed it because my toes suddenly felt hot. And even though I greatly appreciated the Dogfish Head 90 Minute IPA, I really needed water. In fact, even after drinking both bottles of beer my mouth was still so dry that I could barely choke down two leftover chicken nuggets and half a Snickers bar.

At 7:30 P.M., all there was to do was to sit back in the pocket created by my boot prints and try to answer the questions that I had posed to myself.

Why am I up here alone, hunkered down in a tent on the side of a mountain in 17-degree weather? Well, I'm here because I have been going on solo winter backpacking trips for several years. The adventures have afforded me a chance to be alone with my thoughts, to forget about my stressful job, and to experience Nature in a unique fashion. I usually went to Mount Mitchell or Cold Mountain, but this year I decided to do something new: ski backpacking. And Black Balsam seemed the best choice. It had lots of snow and treeless mountain tops and no people. Of course, I discovered that there was one other foolhardy soul brave enough, or stupid enough to be out here, but he didn't plan on spending the night and he stayed on the Parkway. He probably easily skied up to Black Balsam and made a few runs before returning to his vehicle and a steaming thermos of hot chocolate.

Why did I venture off of the Parkway? The trail! I love trails. I love their mystery and adventure. I love the unpredictability of traveling through forests on foot paths. I love the musky smell of the earth and of decomposing leaves. I love to decipher tracks captured in the mud and loose dirt. Which way were they going and how long ago? I love to watch the contour of the hillsides unfold and sweet water springs erupting from beneath moss-covered boulders. I'm mesmerized by raging streams crashing down rock-strewn gashes in the earth. I love the primal feeling of journeying into the unknown, alone – the tingle of danger and fear. I love my reward: recounting the adventure – the highs, the lows, the mental and physical effort, the beauty, and the anxieties. And I revel in misadventures, narrow escapes, and uncertain outcomes. Finally, I love the feeling of accomplishment I get by laying down a challenge, meeting it, and surviving.

Why was I off course? That's simple. The deep snow on the ridge left no trace of a trail and the iced branches blocking the way made it impossible to follow any established course. In the end, I was not where I wanted to be because conditions and gravity coerced me to travel in directions that I wouldn't have chosen on a different day. I like to tell folks that "I ain't never been lost, but I been powerful turned around " and fortunately I've always figured out where I went wrong and made it back home. This trip was no different.

Why did I force myself through the wilderness? Pigheadedness? Yes, I guess. But really, it never occurred to me to stop, or turn around. If nothing else, I am determined. I will accomplish the mission. I will ignore pain and suffering. I will push ahead. I will push myself to my limits. I do it all of the time – running, biking, and climbing. I push myself physically and mentally. Ice climbing is the easiest example. Leading on ice is crazy dangerous and scary as hell. Just getting to the frozen waterfalls is usually physically demanding, my pack with ropes, crampons, ice axes, ice screws, helmet and all of the other necessary gear and clothing weighs about forty pounds. Then, I must traipse through the woods - usually a bushwhack - for up to a couple of miles with varying elevation gains.

Once on the ice, I ascend the frozen water knowing that it will definitely collapse sometime. I just hope it won't come crashing down while I'm on it. The gear I must take up is heavy, maybe twenty pounds. As I climb, I place ice screws I hope will arrest my fall should that happen. I know that a fall could result in some of my very sharp gear puncturing my body. A fall could easily end with me in the ICU or morgue. The whole deal is physically demanding, mentally challenging and just plain stupid. Ice climbing will definitely push you to your limits. The name of the game is control. Control your motions and your emotions.

I worked for a while as an orderly in a hospital where multiple old men who were recovering from heart attacks, or on their death beds due to various illnesses, advised me to "never wait to have fun." It happened so often that I took their advice to heart. It became an integral part of my philosophy.

I decided long ago that I didn't want to live an ordinary life – whatever that means. I didn't want to waste my singular, precious existence living the same mundane, forgettable life as my next door neighbor, only marking time during a 50-year career selling used cars, or managing a wholesale carpet outlet and spending each evening sitting on the couch watching reruns of *The Andy Griffith Show*. I didn't wish to merely plod through the years in a mind-numbing daze. No, I wanted ACTION. Excitement! Adventure! I wanted to have some stories to tell the grandkids. I wanted to stand on the edge of the abyss, thumb my nose at gravity and Satan, narrowly avoid disaster, cheat Death, then return home safely – maybe bruised, but with a unique story that celebrated LIFE.

Additionally, taking real risks forces me to face my true self, to examine my soul, my character. Holding hands with Death gives me an opportunity to evaluate my inner workings, my strengths and fears. Shortcomings are exposed.

False bravado wilts when faced with real physical consequences. Heroes will meet all challenges; fakers will find excuses to avoid risky, dangerous situations. Plus, I told my mother long ago, "Momma, if it's stupid – I can do it!" And I have, a hundred times, or more.

And so, as I rolled and tumbled throughout the long winter night, I pondered and silently debated my situation and plans for the morning. Finally, about midnight, my mind and body succumbed to exhaustion, but I was wracked by a fitful sleep filled with crazy restless dreams and worry. The underlying theme was that I was in a hostile location where a small mistake or injury could mean disaster. I was in a place where rescuers couldn't see me from the air and would never think to investigate on foot. I was alone, weakened, and afraid.

Just before sunrise, my bladder awakened my brain and commanded that I relieve myself. Reluctantly I obeyed. I pulled on my soaking wet boots, zipped up my big bad belay jacket and pulled my ugly hat down tight. I focused my headlamp, unzipped the tent and stepped out into the subfreezing air. I postholed a couple of feet away from the tent and jettisoned the syrupy renal effluent. After assuring that I didn't piss on my boots, I extinguished the light. Magic!

The early morning sky was still inky black except for the brilliant stars that shone through the naked tree top branches. The winter air was crisp and dry. There was no breeze and no sounds other than mine. Perfect isolation.

Guaranteed, very few people have ever stood on this little patch of earth – perhaps only me. As I loitered in the silent stillness, The Struggle, the exhaustion and frustration of the previous day, faded. The blanket of snow reflected the light cast by a billion stars. My eyes adjusted and the miracle that is the forest slowly emerged. It enchanted me, invigorated me. I felt alive. I felt privileged. This is what I came for, a bold adventure. Though not really a life or death skirmish with the elements, it was a noteworthy struggle nonetheless, and it wasn't over yet.

The eastern sky soon offered some hope. An orange smudge appeared in the direction that I was facing. Daybreak. I consulted the map again and determined approximately where I was. From that boundary marker high on the ridge, I had descended several hundred feet and now faced almost due east. If I scooted, crawled and groveled toward the brightening smudge, I should intersect the Black Balsam road and be home free, kinda'. I packed up as quickly as possible and began "the journey: part two" before the sun peeked over the horizon.

In the faint light and 15-degree dawn air, I shouldered the pack and trudged toward the rising sun. Of course, I post-holed with each step and I fell and swore aloud just as I had the day before. And of course, my icy nemesis almost immediately took control of my route forcing me to crawl, saw, and alter any direct pathway toward the brightening horizon. After a few minutes of serpentine travel, while pushing my pack ahead of me under the lowest branches of my prison, I noticed that some of the lowest parts of the laurel and rhododendron had been trimmed. I was on some old path! Up higher, the limbs arched over me forming a distinct tunnel.

I was elated. Here was a tunnel about two and a half feet high and all downhill. I slid on my butt and pulled the pack behind me. Soon, I popped out of the bushes onto a bank that bordered Black Balsam road. In minutes I had traveled half of yesterday's entire distance. I could have cried.

Once on the road, I began skiing again and thanked myself for returning to the ridge top and recapturing the errant ski pole. The road curved gently downhill for about a quarter of a mile, then intersected the Blue Ridge Parkway. I was on my way, but not without difficulty. The crystalline surface offered almost no traction and I've already told you how hard it was to make progress with the worn out skis. I mostly went forward, but I did quite a few splits, my adductors unable to keep the skis from repelling each other until I could no longer balance. Then "plop," I would fall and cuss and laugh out loud at the absurdity of the situation. The pressure was off. I no longer worried about getting lost, being off course, becoming injured and needing a rescue. I was on the Parkway about three or four miles from the truck. I could crawl that distance (as I had already proven) with both legs broken. So I took my time and enjoyed the early morning stillness, the solitude and the most incredible sunrise spectacle I've ever witnessed.

The dim orange smudge slowly expanded. It chased away the black night and the brilliant twinkling heavenly lights. By the time I slid out of the final rhodo tunnel, the eastern sky was painted with reds and orange. The indistinct grey forms of trees were now assuming their normal color of browns and deep green. There were a few clouds low on the horizon, layered as though they had been loosely stacked. The sunrise light shone through the gaps casting beams at various angles that bounced off the icicles. The sun's rays reflected through the thick ice that coated everything. There was a prism effect. At times it was as if I were looking through a kaleidoscope. Unreal colors bent at odd angles.

I took a photograph of the sunrise at about 7:30 A.M. It showed the snow-imprisoned, ice-choked Cradle of Forestry in the Pisgah National Forest. The sun was a few degrees above the horizon. The surrounding sky was a perfect blue miracle. There was a thin line of grayish clouds hovering just above awakening mountains.

The mountains were still shadowed toward me with brilliant highlights riding their ridges and tops. The scene nearest me was a thick forest of leafless wild cherry trees, the ubiquitous rhododendron and laurels, giant Christmas tree shaped balsams and other naked bushes all heavily coated in ice. There were icicles several feet long hanging from some of the branches. Everywhere the sun's rays reflected and refracted; the effect was mesmerizing.

But the most wondrous sight was a "sun dog" or parhelion. This phenomenon occurs as the sun's rays are scattered by ice crystals in the atmosphere. I had never seen it before. The sun seemed to be bordered on the left by a gigantic red sphere while on its right was a brilliant multi-armed exploding star! Awestruck, I watched for 15 minutes until the effect vanished. Then I began skiing again, energized and elated as though I had just witnessed the Gates of Heaven opening for me. "This is what Life is all about!" I shouted to the wilderness. "This is why I struggle. This makes every pain and drop of sweat worth enduring. God, I love being alive!"

I plugged in the iPod and cranked up the Moody Blues, "… here is your dream, and now how does it feel?" I skied back to the truck. I was the luckiest man on Earth.

When I got home, I told my story to my wife and children, detailing all of the trials and tribulations. I showed them the photo of the sun dog and the omnipresent ice and snow. They appreciated the beauty captured in the photos, but shook their heads in disbelief as I detailed the struggle with the skis and ice, of being lost and exhausted. "When will you learn? Why didn't you turn around? Don't you know that you could have been hurt or even killed?" I shook my head, tucked my tail, and put away my gear.

Over the next few days, I told and retold the story to my buddies and workmates. With each rendition, I was forced to answer the same questions about danger and injury. I was forced to hear my answers that downplayed the risks and rationalized my behavior. Finally, after regaling audiences ten or more times and listening to myself confess to pigheadedness and possible stupidity, I reexamined my ordeal, privately and in depth.

Maybe they're right. Maybe I took too big a chance, too many chances. Maybe I shouldn't have. Maybe I should grow up and stop acting so foolish.

I wrestled with the issues for a couple of days. It's true I took some chances in some crazy weather and I had no one to rely on but myself had there been problems. I struggled like never before, I was angry with myself at times, and I was a pitiful wreck when I crawled into the tent. It's true that in some people's minds I pushed well beyond accepted safety and sanity limits. I pondered all of this.

A dim vision brightened into a grand realization.

After much deliberation, I realized that I don't have to be Superman, to pit myself against formidable conditions and life threatening circumstances. I don't have to always forge ahead, to execute the plan unaltered. Adventures should be all about FUN and if something isn't fun, it's okay to stop, change the plan, turn around, do something else. I learned that it isn't a mortal sin to call it a day and go home if conditions aren't right, or if the misery factor out weights the fun factor.

What a revelation. An epiphany!

Oh, I'll probably still court danger and crawl under bushes. I'll get into awkward situations that demand nerves of steel and a hell of a lot of luck in order to survive. But now I've given myself permission to abort any mission and avoid any challenge if the going gets too rough, or if the fun has been replaced by misery.

Airplane Rides

(Excerpt from an imaginary Seinfeld episode)

Jerry: Aaaggh, I've got to go to Cleveland this Friday to do a show.

Elaine: Ohio?

Jerry: Yeah, Ohio. Cleveland Ohio. You know the one.

Elaine: Yeah, I know the one. Hmmm… on an airplane? Are ya going to fly?

Jerry: Yes on an airplane! It's too far to drive.

Elaine: Yuck, I hate planes!

Jerry: Yeah, me too. I hate airplanes. (pause) I hate airplanes. I hate airports. I hate the schedules and the waiting around and the …

George: And the germs, Jerry! What about all of those germs flying around. People hackin' and coughing and wiping their noses, leaving snotty wadded-up tissues all over the place. God, it's a cesspool, Jerry! Literally, a breeding ground of filth and disease, for pneumonia and hepatitis, for swine flu and probably other diseases that don't even have names yet.

Jerry: OK, OK, alright already!

Kramer: Yeah. Oh, and the people, Jerry. What about the people! Ya gotta sit beside people, Jerry. Somebody you don't even know. And they might have a cold!

George: Yes! They could be sick. What if they're sick, Jerry? You could get sick.

Elaine: And they're gonna want to talk. They always want to talk, Jerry – especially when they find out you're a comedian. You're famous.

Jerry: No! No! No! I can't do it! I can't!! You're right, they always want to talk! But I don't want to talk. I never know what to say.

George: And if you start talking when you first sit down then ya have to talk all during the flight. It'll be endless.

Elaine: Yes, endless, mindless, boring, monotonous, meaningless, <u>STUPID</u> chitchat.

Jerry: Oohhh, this is horrible! You're all right. There'll be this big, humongous sweaty guy with halitosis, or worse, maybe garlic-onion breath. He'll want to tell me all about his boyhood on the farm getting up before sunrise, milking cows and feeding chickens, his eight sisters and his high school letter jacket, his four kids and their summer vacation to Disneyland and the time Aunt Sadie slipped on the ice and broke her hip.

Kramer: Yeah, Jerry – and he'll be a close talker. And he'll want to know what you do for a living and then he'll want you to tell some jokes and he'll announce to everyone on the plane that you're a comedian and they'll all want your autograph!

Jerry: Oh, god! Oh, god! I can't take it! I can't do it! I hate airplanes! I've got to call my agent right now and cancel!!

***

Okay, so I'm not Larry David. But I have had some pretty interesting experiences in airports and on planes. Here are three true stories involving air travel and my miserable luck. The third tale is not politically correct and is disgusting. So, if you're the sensitive sort, easily offended by humor that focuses on others' imperfections, frailties, or misfortune then you probably should skip that one.

No Guns, No Knives

My problems with air travel began in 1984, but I wasn't traveling by air, my parents were. I had moved to Missoula, Montana and my parents had come to visit. We'd had a super time in the western mountains and I was feeling frisky and jovial when I accompanied them to the Missoula airport for their return flight to Asheville.

Back in those days, Missoula was a sleepy little town with a sleepy little airport that had only one runway. I think that there may have been only two flights per day.

I'm almost certain that they didn't even have radar yet, just some guy in the two-story "tower" with a spotting scope or binoculars. He would set his alarm clock so he could get out of his La-Z-Boy swivel recliner a few minutes before the flight's scheduled arrival and confirm over the P.A. system that, "Northwest flight number so-'n-so is about to arrive on runway #1. All exiting passengers may be met a gate A."

Anyway, on this particularly fine day as we entered the terminal, I noticed a small sign that I'd never seen before. It was an 8x10-inch sticker pasted to the glass door that read:

NO GUNS.
NO KNIVES.
NO FALSE STATEMENTS

It struck me as odd and so I commented to my father – in a normal tone and with conversational volume, but in a facetious manner, "Hey dad, I've got a false statement in my pocket." And I snickered. Well, the lady with the clipboard overheard me. She went straight to the security guard – yep, the big buzz cut humorless guy with the gun. And he made a beeline for me.

Now, I'm no Einstein, but I did manage to learn a couple of years before to never argue with the guy who has the gun. Without a smile and with authority, he ordered me to get out of the airport. "Get out of the terminal now, mister!" I started to explain that I was just joking and that I didn't really have a false statement in my pocket. But these two didn't have any sense of humor. They wouldn't even let me hug my parents good-bye. I was shooed away like blowflies on Mother Theresa's corpse.

In retrospect, I realize that their actions were most likely part of a national knee jerk response to airline hijackings and terrorists' activities. No joking matter.

Airport: 1. Mike: zero

The Boarding Pass

Round two occurred in 1993. Yes, I avoided airports for ten years – statute of limitations and all. In '93 I had a girlfriend who was working in Tucson, Arizona while I had a job in Colorado. I visited her once. It was April and hotter than a habanera enema. I had a four-day weekend, so I had to fly. This time I didn't piss off airport security, thank goodness. The airline carrier pissed me off. But it was my own fault – I guess.

I was seated in 13D, a window seat, and I kept my eye on the passengers who were boarding, who might be my row mates. There were the usual businessmen with briefcases and folded newspapers. There were white-haired grandmothers with sickly-sweet perfume, pancake make-up, ruby red lipstick, and huge crocheted purses. I saw a couple of pimply-faced college students wearing baggy cotton sweatpants and hooded warm-up jackets sporting school logos. And of course, the huge bald-headed cowboy with a 10-gallon Stetson, a black leather duster, and a river of sweat dripping off of his forehead, who most assuredly would be crammed into the seat beside me.

With trepidation and while holding my breath I watched as Doc Holliday lumbered down the aisle. He inspected my row and its numeric designation, but kept going. Somehow he was not scheduled to sit beside me, squeezing me into the bulkhead and annoying me with cowboy stories and struggling post-apnea snores.

Finally, just as the flight attendant announced that the last passengers had boarded and that we should all take our seats and buckle up, two very handsome young ladies made their way down the aisle. I held my breath and prayed. Surely God would smile on me and seat these two angels next to me. He didn't.

But He did seat them in the row behind me! I was left in my row all alone. (These were the days before the airlines' economic collapse, before overbooking and less leg room, when one might have space enough to spread out a little during a flight.) Anyway, somehow these two gifts from Heaven decided to take an interest in me and we began a conversation that lasted from Denver to Salt Lake City.

I don't recall their names any more and they may not have ever told me, but I do recall their faces – young, smooth skin, lightly adorned with the perfect amount of make-up. Both had gorgeous, lustrous, flowing blond hair; they were thin, athletically built and with ample bosom, straight pearly-white teeth, and no rings on their left hands. I was mesmerized. I couldn't believe my luck!

I would have changed seats and sat beside them if I could have, but 14A and B were occupied by two of the aforementioned grandmothers. So, I wiggled and squirmed and twisted around in my seat in order to observe the girls through the gap between the seatbacks while we chatted. I even reclined my seat to improve the view. They were on holiday, going backpacking with friends in the Grand Canyon. And so we talked about hiking, mountains, adventures, places we had either been, or wanted to go. It was lovely. I didn't want the flight to ever end. Nirvana, most assuredly must be just like this. But of course the journey did end. The plane approached the Salt Lake runway and I had to return my "seat back to the upright position, stow all carry-ons in the overhead compartment, or underneath the seat and buckle the seatbelt."

When the plane landed, our conversation ceased. I returned to thoughts of seeing my girlfriend. I hadn't seen her for several weeks and I had never been to Tucson, so there was reason for further excitement. But in the back of my mind I did kinda wish that those two golden-haired nymphs would take my hand in the terminal and kidnap me for a desert trip never to be forgotten. We exchanged good-byes and best wishes as we exited the airplane and a little piece of my adolescent heart broke as we parted company.

I was still swimmy-headed when I arrived at the gate where I would board the plane to Tucson. I checked in with the lady at the desk.

"Boarding pass," she said flatly.

I reached into my back pocket. I had put it there – where I couldn't lose it – prior to sitting in 13D. And yep, you guessed it. It wasn't there. It wasn't there, or in any of my pockets, or in my pack. It was gone. Somehow with all the wiggling and squirming and ogling it must have fallen out. Well, no problem, I thought. The clipboard lady has got my name, reservation number and seat assignment on her list and I have my I.D. Problem solved.

"I'm sorry ma'am. I seem to have misplaced it, but I do have my I.D. and you can check it against your list."

"I'm sorry, sir, but you must have that pass, or you can't get on this plane."

"You're kiddin'."

"Nope!"

"Well can you call the plane that I just got off of and see if anyone has found it? I was sitting in 13D. It probably fell out of my pocket around there."

"Nope, I can't do that."

"Really? Please?"

"No, sir. Policy, you know."

I was flabbergasted. I was furious. I felt like stomping my feet and yelling obscenities. I felt like announcing my plight to the crowd, shaming the airline and its policies, and enlisting whatever help I could get. I wanted to choke clipboard lady, but I didn't.

Easy, Mike. Take a deep breath. Count to ten. Mental images of big burly men with guns and skinny little me in handcuffs being roughly escorted out of the terminal. Cast out onto the highway. Would the streets of SLC treat me kindly? Probably not. I don't like sleeping on the sidewalk – did that in Portugal – it sucked. And I've never cared for the accommodations that the county offers: the metal bars and a cell full of disreputable hooligans.

"Well then, what do I do – Ma'am?"

"Sir, you'll have to find that boarding pass, or buy another ticket."

"What?!!"

"Or you can pay fifty dollars and we can reissue a pass."

"You're kiddin'. Fifty bucks?"

"Yes, sir, administrative fees."

Well, I didn't have fifty dollars. So I wrote her a check and prayed that my girlfriend would loan me the cash to cover it. Clipboard lady gladly accepted my worthless check and handwrote a new boarding pass. Then she checked it against her list.

"Yep, you're right here, seat 17B." She handed me the pass and said, "Thank you for flying Northwest. Have an enjoyable flight and a nice day!"

Baloney! I boarded the plane and had a nice day fuming about how I just got screwed.

Airlines: 2. Mike still zero.

Mister Huge

My most recent experience on an airplane has turned out to be the most disturbing and the most disgusting.

I should have guessed that this trip would be memorable by the way our plans began. In early December 2010, we had arranged our flights from Asheville to Steamboat Springs. Around Christmas, the airline notified us of changes to our itinerary that called for very short layovers in Charlotte and Denver. The times between flights were so short that there would be no way to make it from one plane to the next. And, of course, if there were any flight delays, we would certainly not be on the connecting flight.

Kelly called the airline. After a frustrating 90 minutes, she got the flights rearranged. Then, as recommended by the airline, the day before our scheduled departure Kelly accessed our itinerary to confirm the plans and check in on line. Guess what? The plans to come home – Steamboat to Asheville were in order, but there was no evidence of our itinerary from Asheville to the ski resort. My wife was <u>not</u> happy. Another lengthy, maddening phone call ensued. She finally got it straightened out but we could not all sit together – an inauspicious start to a once-in-a-lifetime family vacation.

We awakened at 3:30 A.M. with trepidation and went to the airport.

Here comes the politically incorrect part.

In my opinion, there is no excuse for being nasty – dirty, funky, unwashed, partially rotting, decaying, and obnoxiously odiferous – nasty because you choose to ignore basic care of yourself. I can not tolerate lazy, foul, disgusting people who do not care about themselves or their impact on anyone else. Unless your arms, hands and fingers DO NOT work, there is no excuse for filthy.

Sooo… We boarded the airplane headed to Denver from Charlotte. I was scheduled to sit in 7C while my children held tickets for 6A and C. My wife sat in 6D. The kids scooted into their row and Kelly took her assigned seat. I, however, discovered that my seat was occupied. And you guessed it. The fellow in my seat was humongous! Not only that, but he was detestably, disgustingly nasty.

At first glance, I really could not believe my eyes. This guy was 420 pounds if he was an ounce. Not only that, but he appeared to be a caricature of some twisted Hunchback of Notre Dame. His nappy brown and grey hair stood at all angles, uncombed, greasy, and unwashed. His face was a frightening mask of large flaky eczematous skin and various open sores. He hadn't shaved his beard in more than a week, the stubble only partially hiding the remains of some type of food or drink consumed earlier and gripping the skin flakes that were promising to avalanche at any moment. His eyes were shielded by bushy brows that held back an inordinate volume of dried skin chips. Additionally, the windows to his soul were set at different angles so that he could see around corners and I had no idea which eye to focus on when I spoke to him. His left eyelid drooped – covering most of that iris – kinda like Popeye's, while the right was lazily open. The conjunctiva of each was swollen, ruby-red, and threatening to leak blood. I wasn't certain if he could see at all because his eyes were cloudier than Irish skies in January. Cataracts and arcus senilis (white rings around the pupil) I said to myself as I grimaced, shuddered, and inhaled to speak to him. Ooo, bad idea! Great God in heaven! What is that horrible odor? I noticed that his exposed skin had a pale grayish hue, a reptilian texture, dry and unhealthy. A renal patient? They exude an ammonia scent sometimes – the poor pitiful guy, my inner voice whispered. I quickly studied his arms. There was no evidence of any hemodialysis fistulae, maybe he uses peritoneal dialysis.

I nodded to him as he looked up at me with his half-dead eyes. "I'm supposed to be in that seat," I said. He mumbled almost incoherently that he had to use a wheelchair and it was hard to move over, but as he spoke he began to scoot to his left. His ticket called for him to sit in 7A. Blowing and huffing, he pushed down with his pockmarked arms and dragged his massive butt across the faux leather seats. His progress hampered by his bulk and <u>four</u> bags of Chick-fil-A grease bombs which were in his lap. The hoard of boarding passengers pressed down on me. I could feel their anxiety, their impatience, their anger escalating because I was holding up their progress.

As Mr. Huge moved across the row the odor became more apparent. It was much stronger than I had initially realized. It was as strong as the stench from a baby diaper pail filled with dirty, urine-soaked, crappy diapers, and unemptied for a month. God, this guy reeked! Worse yet, after he moved out of my seat, I noticed that he had left a small puddle of pee!

You've got to be kiddin' me! I quickly scanned the plane hoping to find a flight attendant close by who could wipe out, wash out, disinfect, or burn my seat and replace it with a fresh one. But none could be found. The crowd pressed. Innumerable sets of "the evil eye" bored into me. "Sit, you dolt, you're holding up progress." The pressure mounted. My heart sank. My brow wrinkled and my lips turned up slightly in a sickened, defeated little smile, what a story this will make! I know that I'm being punished and I know that I deserve it, but this'll be really gross. I sat. I'll burn the pants.

The crowd squeezed by as soon as I began to sit, nearly toppling me onto the still mumbling troll. And as I sat, the putrid miasma of unwashed crevices, folds and holes overpowered me. A dense cloud of acrid, acidic stench burned my nostrils and assaulted my senses. My eyes began to water and I retched a little. Control yourself. Do not vomit.

All the while, Mr. Huge continued to talk to me, mumbling, droning on and on. I had no idea of what he was saying. And he stopped in 7B. Oh no! I nearly panicked – I don't think I can sit directly beside this rancid sewer slob. He'll spill over into my seat. I'll have to touch his disgusting clothes, and maybe his decaying flesh. His fetid odor will be too close, too strong. I'm sure I will vomit. He'll mumble incessantly and I'll have to pay attention and reply to his inane ramblings. And I will be forced to look at his wretched twisted face. But which eye? He will shed dermatitis flakes like autumn leaves in a hurricane. God, I'm sorry – I promise to repent!

Fortunately, 7B was just a rest stop. The skuzball moved into the window seat where he was supposed to be. Now I couldn't tell if he was actually paralyzed or just so damn fat that he couldn't walk and needed a wheelchair. And as he scooched over, his filthy, stained trousers nearly came off. I was relieved that he was at least a bit farther away. Still the sight and smell were overpowering. I tried to be small, take small breathes, hold my breath, ignore the locker room urinal odor. Nothing helped.

After a couple of minutes, during which time Mr. Huge was muttering about being eight years old and doing something that I could not understand, a young woman eyeballed our row and took her seat in 7B. Oh, what a relief! What luck – for me. At least there will be someone else breathing this foul air, filtering it with their lungs, exhaling diluted funk, someone between me and him (how selfish), watering down the experience. Someone to share this agony with – poor thing. She'll never be the same after this three-hour torture.

Within seconds, while I'm still standing to allow miss 7B to get situated, another young lady approached. She studied the row numbers and settled on 6B, the middle seat, right between my two children. She hesitated momentarily – just long enough for my brain to formulate a scheme and my tongue to deliver it in the same instant.

"Miss, would you mind switching seats with me so I can sit with my kids?"

"Oh, of course, sir. Certainly."

I soared with excitement, the hope of new found freedom and then wilted in embarrassment, shame and guilt. I had escaped my prison but sentenced an innocent to my former misery. I had broken some moral obligation, some cosmic law that demands that we should protect the young and unsuspecting from all of the evil and vulgar things in this universe. I had cleverly swapped my disgusting position on that plane for a far better one and had tricked this blameless child into suffering one of the most offensive punishments imaginable.

While she struggled with the overhead compartment, I shot into 6B, laid my claim, welded myself to that spot so that no amount of cajoling, complaining, or pleading could wrench me out, or force me back into 7C. Yes, I felt guilty – what a sneaky unconscionable ratfink. I really did feel bad about it, but I grew up Catholic – I know all about guilt, I'd get over it. It's a dog-eat-dog world! Actually, I had done the poor young thing a favor. She will have learned a valuable lesson: never trust anyone. Well, maybe not.

Anyway, I sat between Nathan and Kylie for the ride to Denver, but the stench was so strong that my improved position wasn't much help. Both children were aware of the offensive stink and quietly asked me about it.

I whispered to 7-year old Kylie, in a polite manner, that the gentleman behind us had some kind of problem and that he peed in his pants. But to Nathan, who was on my left side and directly in front of Mr. Huge, I was more blunt. "The nasty guy right behind you hasn't bathed or changed his clothes in a month. Plus, he peed in his pants and that's what you smell." My son snickered a little bit, then returned to an expression of incredulous disgust, squinted eyes, pinched nostrils, and wrinkled brow. He buried his nose in his cupped hands and leaned as far forward as possible to increase his distance from the source of the nauseating fumes. We both chuckled. It was surely going to be a long ride.

Kylie curled up as best she could and closed her eyes. We had awakened very early and were all still sleepy. But Nathan and I managed to smile and wink at one another, as normal boys do when faced with disgustingly vile affairs like letting farts in church, or watching siblings step in dog doo-doo. But we couldn't keep it up for long. Really, our situation was not funny in the least and within a couple of minutes both of us fell into a chasm of hopeless despair. We were trapped and we both knew it. We stopped joking around and kept our noses poked into our cupped hands. We did our best to seal out the miserable air, but it was of no use. The aroma of deep-fried airport Chick-fil-A blended with rotten diaper pail ammonia funk penetrated our open fist filters. We wound up simply looking at each other in disgust and despair. Three hours, three hours. Could we survive this torment for three hours? Waterboarding, bamboo under fingernails, or hot pokers in the eyes seemed more appealing.

The plane was about to take off.

"Ladies and gentlemen, please return your seat back to the full upright position and make sure that your tray table is locked into its stowed position. Additionally, please fasten your safety belts and secure them tightly around your waist." The flight attendants walked up and down the aisles and checked all of the passengers. Mr. Huge was not in compliance and the attendant reminded him, ordered him, and finally, kind of yelled at him.

We had to watch. The poor fellow was so big and clumsy that he couldn't collect all those food bags and raise the tray table. After the fourth warning and over his objections, the exasperated stewardess demanded the bags and snatched them away. Still, he couldn't move fast enough, or coordinate his movements. We started to taxi. His tray was still down and his belt remained unfastened.

A second and then a third attendant joined the fray. They all admonished him in unison. I actually felt a little sorry for him. It reminded me of boot camp where three drill instructors would surround you, nose-to-nose and screaming mouth to each ear. They would hurl obscenities, berate and frighten you into a quaking gelatinous mass of submission. One attendant held the food bags while one fixed the tray table. The third fetched a seat belt extension and helped apply it properly. As they got close enough to help the man the expression on each woman's face was priceless. Angry, glaring eyes and wrinkled finger-pointing brows quickly transformed into pop-eyed, snurled-nosed, OMG!-I-can't-believe-it expressions. Nathan and I snickered again, but quickly returned to our air filtering strategy.

Mostly, we commiserated nonverbally, but at some low point, Nathan looked to me as his FATHER, the one with experience, the guy who KNOWS, the man with the answer.

"Isn't there anything that we can do, dad?"

The plane was full – not an empty seat to be had. There was simply nowhere to go. I explained this as his eyes teared.

I almost said that we could smear dog shit under our noses and make things better, but I didn't. But I did offer this suggestion, "Let's ask mom for some gum and shove a piece up each nostril." He chuckled a little and then resumed the position.

The flight was long and miserable. I felt sorry for my children; I felt sorry for myself. I really felt sorry for the girls sitting right beside Mr. Huge. Woe is me. What could be worse? Oh yeah, soon our humongous aromatic friend will fall asleep, drop his goliath head onto his chest and become apneic. He'll struggle for untold minutes with intensive chest rocking, turn purple, hover just above death, but ultimately generate enough negative pressure to vacuum some air past the pounds of obstructive tissue in his throat to inhale with snores that will rock the plane, awaken him and frighten everyone within earshot.

After that, some young cranky child will begin to cry inconsolably for hours. Olfactory and auditory nerve overstimulation will take its toll and drive me insane. I'll never even see Denver, much less Steamboat Springs. Oh, woe is me.

After a couple of hours, Kylie needed a potty break. I accompanied her to the rear of the plane where the restrooms and the flight attendants where located. While my daughter peed, the flight attendants and I chatted. They apologized for 7A's size and odor. I laughed and replied, "Yes, he does reek and he's totally nasty. He was in my seat initially and when I asked him to move over, he left a puddle of pee in my seat."

The attendants gasped. "He what?" said one.

"You've got to be kidding!" said the other.

"No I'm not," I replied. "And I had to sit in it!"

The women's faces flushed and they pressed me for the whole story. Before Kylie finished in the bathroom, I summarized my brief experience in row 7 and I told them about switching seats and about how Mr. Huge's pungent and vile sticky essence permeated our area, disgusted us, nauseated us, and thoroughly tortured us.

"I've changed hundreds of baby diapers. I've washed hundreds of adults' butts in the hospital and nursing homes. I've cleaned out horse stalls – the crap two feet deep, a year old, and infested with maggots. I've mucked out broken, overflowing septic tanks. But I have never smelled anything worse than that guy! I've even helped a homeless guy who lived in a dumpster and he didn't smell as bad as Mr. 7A."

The attendants reeled in disgust. Did the blonde actually retch? (I love to make people squirm.) They scrambled to make amends. Snacks for the kids were immediately offered along with energetic, heartfelt "I'm so sorrys!" and "someone should have recognized this problem and kept him from boarding!" All of their flapping around was pretty entertaining. Loaded with our reparation larder of mini Chips Ahoy! and M&Ms, we returned to our seats and the poisonous gas hell. As we took our seats, I noted that Mr. Huge was fast asleep, his legs splayed, his necrotic arms limp – the right one pressing on miss 6B's left thigh, his double chin resting on his chest. My heart sank. Any moment now the mounds of redundant throat tissue will occlude his airway and he will begin his purple-faced, chest-rocking, sleep apnea breathing interrupted by explosive 150-decibel snores.

I warned Nathan and challenged him to surreptitiously photograph Mr. Huge with his new iPod Touch. He did. And while the picture is worth a thousand words, it does not fully capture the gravity of the situation. Nor can it convey the olfactory trauma.

Before long, the flight attendant girls were back. In hushed tones, so as to not awaken our sleeping garbage heap, they once again apologized to me and the two girls in row seven and they gave each of us a small form and pencil. They asked us to explain in writing what had happened with regard to Mr. Huge and his perma-funk. They would report the situation and find the villain responsible for allowing such a nasty person on the plane. The airline would pay for our laundering, or new trousers if they were beyond repair. Somebody knew that this guy was filthy and reeked and shouldn't have been allowed on a plane. Someone was to blame. Someone should have prevented this horrible situation. Someone was going to pay!

Inwardly, I chuckled. Hell, yes, someone knew. As I boarded I saw Mr. Huge's double-wide wheelchair parked just outside the aircraft in the jetway. Beside it sat the extra narrow wheelchair owned by the airline. It fits in the aircraft's aisle (because regular wheelchairs are too wide) and is used to board disabled passengers. Somebody helped Mr. Huge squeeze into the teeny chair, pushed him onto the plane, down the aisle, and levered him into my seat. Hell, yeah, somebody knew he was nasty. There was no way anyone could be within ten feet of this guy and not be repulsed by his rotting odor and disgusted by his filthy clothes. Hell, yeah, somebody knew all about this abhorrent, malodorous, enormous pig! But most likely, they deposited him in my seat and immediately raced to the nearest restroom to vomit and sterilize themselves. Or maybe they suffocated to death before they could alert the airline and Homeland Security.

Anyway, the remainder of the flight was interminably miserable, but uneventful. And thankfully, since we were in the front of the plane, we exited within minutes of the hatch being opened. Mr. Huge slept through the attendants' apology session and for the remainder of the flight and even though a baby did cry, it wasn't for long.

That's the end of this story except to say that I've had a hell of a good time recounting the episode to all of my friends and family and comparing our experience with other folk's worst airline experiences. To date, riding with Mr. Huge has won, or lost, as the most revolting plane ride. And apparently, I am the only human stupid enough to sit in a puddle of someone else's piss.

Airlines?: 3. Mike still zero!
I agree with imaginary Seinfeld. I hate planes.

Mother Theresa

If you told me this story, I absolutely would not believe it.

...I'm supposed to be dead.

We were driving home, west on 64, when we passed the sign we always made fun of:

MOTHER THERESA
PSYCHIC
Palm Reading, Fortunes, High Colonics
next right

"Let's pull in, see what it's all about," Kelly said with a giggle.

"Naw, it's a waste of time and money – just a bunch a crap."

"Ah, come on, it'll be fun. My treat. Ya know you've always wanted to see what it's all about – 'specially that high colonic."

"Right, like I'm gonna pay some old lady for an enema."

She tugged on the steering wheel. I stepped on the brake and pulled off the highway.

The empty gravel lot was big enough for three cars. The structure had begun as a Philips 66 gas station, the ancient, rusted sign still standing, mostly covered in kudzu. For a decade it housed a fruit stand selling apples, melons, local honey, and boiled peanuts. For the past three years, the single story building wore a sign on the roof advertising the psychic. The peeling whitewashed clapboard was given a fresh coat of pink and black paint and strings of multi-colored Christmas tree lights bordered the eves and window frames, winking at motorists as they hurried past on their way to Edneyville and beyond.

We were met at the door by an ancient pale woman.

"Welcome, welcome friends. I trust you are well. I am Mother Theresa."

"Yes, hello," Kelly replied as she reached for the old woman's extended hand. "I'm..."

"No, please," the psychic interrupted. She paused. "Your first names begin with letters from the middle of the alphabet, interrupted by your surname's."

Kelly and I eyed each other. A clever trick I told myself, but amazing.

"Yes, how'd you know?" asked my wife.

"Ahh, and you've been playing a dangerous game by the lake. Something that requires strength and skill."

My eyebrows raised, but I figured she'd seen the chalk dust on our fingernails and concluded we'd been rock climbing, which was correct. How shrewd.

Mother Theresa kept Kelly's hand, turned it over and examined her palm. The old woman's eyes grew wide and she smiled.

"What do ya see?"

"Ahh, for that young lady you must come into the parlor." She turned and stepped though a thick curtain of colorful beads into a darkened room sweet with incense. A sign above the door displayed the prices of her services.

Kelly smiled, took my hand and said, "Come on, this'll be fun."

I hesitated, rolled my eyes, then we followed.

The dim parlor held a round table and three chairs; there was one window, no other doors, and no Mother Theresa. We studied each other's surprise. I peeled back the heavy window curtain – not behind there, but the view almost knocked me down, I lost my breath.

"Com'ere quick, look at this!"

Kelly peeked. We both saw the top of my truck as though looking down from the third story. Her head whipped around, eyes locked onto mine, our disbelief ricocheted – impossible.

"Sit please," Mother Theresa softly commanded.

We almost fell on the floor. Where had she come from? The beads in the doorway were undisturbed, we'd heard no noise. She'd simply appeared and unbelievably was now wearing completely different clothes and clownish make-up. Moments ago she was a pale old lady dressed for gardening; now, she looked like a sorceress.

She studied Kelly's palm, "You are a very happy woman, strong and intelligent. You have no children now, but will soon be blessed. You'll live a long and satisfying life."

What a bogus, ambiguous declaration I thought, but Kelly was eight weeks pregnant.

"You are from the North and found love in the South. You have a twin brother who lives in Ohio."

Our disbelief filled the room and threatened to suffocate us.

"How in the world could you know that?"

"It's all here, in the lines and there's more."

"No. I don't want to know any more. Read Michael's."

The psychic took my hands, turned them and looked puzzled.

"I scraped them up earlier, cheese-grated 'em falling off a rock climb."

She smiled, reached beneath the table, produced a deck of Tarot cards, shuffled them and turned one over: Poseidon and a tower.

Without looking up she said, "Disaster."

She turned another and covered it with her palm, "The sun and moon will share the sky."

"What does that mean?"

"Shhh!" She turned another: the grim reaper? And a black bird on his shoulder. "Your folly shall be waiting – waiting too long. Follow the ravens, fly as they do."

What?

Kelly and I exchanged inquiring glances. Mother Theresa took the bottom card flipped it over, pondered, turned it face down then said, "Place your left hand on the card, gently – do not breathe as you do."

I smiled, held my breath, and obeyed her command. She placed her left hand on mine, lifted it.

"You may breathe now." She turned the card face up. It was a completely different picture – the Death card. She didn't explain. Unnerved, we paid and left.

As we drove away we teased about the readings, about the vagueness and precision and what a great showman the old woman was. Most puzzling was how she vanished and reappeared in the parlor. What a great trick.

"I'm gonna tell some of my buddies to stop in there. I'll even pay. I'd love to know what she tells 'em, if she's as clever with say…Wikoff or Ian," I said.

"I'm totally amazed she guessed Kyle lived in Ohio. How could she do that?"

"I have absolutely no idea," I replied.

"Whatcha think about those Tarot cards? I know it's all some kind of trick, or something, but I'll still worry about that death card for a while."

"Not me. She's good, I'll give ya that, but I'm not gonna obsess over it. I'm still climbing and biking and …"

"Yeah, yeah, I know." She slipped her hand into mine and turned up the music.

Two weeks later I was still alive and hadn't had any close calls, but Kelly insisted I drive to a conference in Savannah instead of flying. We had a friendly disagreement. My point: driving takes at least five hours, flying maybe three with a stop in Atlanta. She countered that I'd save money, wouldn't need a rental car, and would avoid challenging the death card.

"You said Mother Theresa was right on with Wikoff's reading, even predicted he'd drive his tractor into the creek."

"Yeah, she did guess he worked in a hospital, but he didn't get hurt rolling the tractor and that prediction was really vague – could've been almost anything, 'wheels and water and blood' could've been a bike wreck, or skinned knuckles working on his car."

"Would ya do it for me anyway? At least you'll have control of the car, not rely on the pilot, or traffic controllers. Please?"

Next morning I jumped in my truck and headed to Savannah. On the south side of Columbia SC, I decided to take the direct route: Highway 321, the Savannah Highway. "This'll confuse the old witch, the Death Card will be looking for me on I-95 and I'll be way over here going 55mph and stopping at red lights in every podunk, redneck, backwater cesspool for the next 150 miles," I said out loud and laughed.

Forty-five minutes later, just outside of Denmark SC, I had to stop at a railroad crossing. A Norfolk Southern with a zillion cars crept by whistling and squeaking. I could've walked faster. I dialed Kelly.

"Where ya at?" I asked.

"Up on the Parkway getting ready to run with the dog."

"Beautiful day for that, wish I was there."

"It's so beautiful. You won't believe what I'm looking at. The sky is so blue and I can see the moon ever so faintly just above the mountains," she remarked.

"Wow, I'm sittin' here waitin' for the slowest train in history to go by," I grumbled.

"Across the interstate?"

"No, I decided to take a different route, confuse fate."

"I see," she said mockingly.

"It's been raining and a second ago a lightning bolt hit so close I thought I was a goner. It even scared the birds on the power line, they flew like…"

"Michael! Get out of the truck! Run!"

"What?"

"Just do it. Do it now!" she commanded.

It seemed stupid, but she was frantic. I couldn't drive away anyhow, two cars in front and one behind me. I threw open my door and ran across the highway. As I jumped into the ditch I saw the Death Card coming for me. It was a speeding 18-wheeler going way too fast. He couldn't stop in time on the rain slick road. He jammed his brakes, blew the horn, slowed to maybe 30 mph, and plowed into the line of cars. Mine and the last one burst into flames. The cars in front crumpled and twisted. The one nearest the train was forced under a boxcar and knocked sideways. The semi careened off the car behind mine and rolled into the ditch opposite me. I was still on the phone with Kelly who heard the commotion.

"Michael! What was that? Was that an explosion?"

I was breathing so hard I could barely talk, "Oh my God, yes! A semi just plowed into the truck, it's crushed and on fire! I gotta call 911!"

"Wait!"

I hung up and called the cops.

I never made it to the conference; Kelly picked me up at the police station in Denmark and drove us home. I was totally freaked out. Two people in the car behind my truck died in the fiery crash, all the others in front were injured badly and I'd have been killed. My truck was squashed and had also burst into flames. I would've been trapped inside and roasted.

I thanked Kelly and asked, "Why on earth did ya think I should jump out of the truck?"

"The signs – they all came together. I saw the moon during the day and you were waiting and waiting on the train. When you said that birds flew away after the lightning, Mother Theresa's prediction of disaster flashed in my mind. If you waited too long disaster would strike. She was right!"

Incredible, an old lady's mumbo jumbo and Kelly's quick thinking my saved my life.

Absolutely unbelievable.

Memories of Boot Camp

My memoirs can't be complete without detailing at least some of the wild tales from my Parris Island adventure. While I will attempt to put a humorous spin on these events, I understand that many mothers loaded their sons onto a Greyhound bus as cocky, self-assured bad-asses only to collect them several weeks later from the bus station twitching, broken, nervous wrecks, pale and blubbering shells of quivering flesh with faces that approximated their sons, but deportment more closely resembling asylum escapees.

Harsh, but realistic – I stood at attention and witnessed previously "normal" youths turned to jelly and discharged warped, ruined, unviable. I pity them and pray that somehow through the years they've healed and regained the sanity that was chased away by sadistic drill instructors and a system that tormented us all to the point of needing to seek retribution somehow, to kill when allowed.

Whew! That was heavy.

Okay, my pre-exposure to Marine Corps boot camp was at the AFEEs station in Charlotte NC. Maybe 50 seventeen and eighteen-year olds lined up to be examined by the doctor. We toed a straight red line, stood shoulder to shoulder, dropped our shorts, got a finger in each inguinal canal. "Turn your head and cough, boy." And our grocery holes checked for hemorrhoids. Then, the wobbly, inebriated physician inspected our teeth and throats with a flashlight. I passed muster, as did everyone else in the room. I'll bet a shovel would've been approved for enlistment that day.

An old school bus delivered us to Parris Island at midnight in early September 1975. My first vision of our new home included a buck private giving us the finger as we rolled past his guard shack. He hated us. He hated everything. Given the chance he'd murder his mother.

The bus groaned to a halt beside the oldest buildings on the island, exhausted wooden barracks erected during WWI. The angriest man alive stood at the bus's door and screamed full force. He swung fists that found heads and necks and fleeing backs as we sprinted to stand at attention on sets of yellow footprints stenciled on the pavement.

After a short, expletive-filled speech that left no doubt as to his sanity and the torture he would inflict should we fail to follow instructions exactly, we ran into the barracks where a hundred other recruits were at attention. As I ascended the stairs and crossed the threshold I glimpsed my first casualty: a big-bearded, long-haired dude, standing rod straight, passed out, collapsed, cracked his head open on the hardwood floor, and split the rear of his pants. He wore those pants several days, underwear smiling through the huge hole.

For an hour we stood at attention, trembling as Staff Sgt. Killer and Cpl. Cannibal cursed us, berated us, and promised unimaginable pain if we screwed up. We were their property, more disgusting than a diarrhea milkshake and more putrid than gonorrhea dripping from… Well, you get the picture. They hated us, but with luck, would let us live through the night. We were assigned bunks and put to bed fully clothed at 1A.M.

At 3:30 A.M. the lights came on, the sergeants screamed for us to get out of our racks, toe the black line, and stand at attention. They launched metal trash cans. I flashed into place and had to duck as a Frisbeed trash can lid nearly found my head. It was a long scary day filled with threats and abuses. We stood at attention for long periods as we were instructed, inspected, and mentally disassembled, the first stage in replacing our weak civilian ethos with Marine Corps killer ideology, the first hours of turning little boys into men.

My memories are now riddled with holes, so much has happened since then, but I'll tell a few anecdotes and throw in a couple snippets.

The first day, those who smoked were stripped of their cigarettes, but two of the guys kept theirs – of course they were discovered. All hell broke loose. The offenders were brought before the platoon, verbally abused, smacked around with punches to the belly and arms (no visible bruises), and made to eat their remaining cigarettes, filters and all, with a half a canteen of water while standing at attention. One recruit ate 18, the other 14, the rest of us watched in silence. I vowed not to screw up.

My best friend, Mike McCoy and I had joined at the same time and had been placed in the same platoon along with another high school buddy, Michael Hill. McCoy became the guide and eventually, I became the first squad leader. Michael Hill remained a regular Joe. McCoy's and my positions were ones of pseudo-authority and responsibility.

They brought with them accolades and troubles. We marched at the front of the platoon, kept the appropriate pace, rhythm, and arrow-straight direction. We were also saddled with assuring platoon discipline and prowess; we were held responsible for any screw-up by any member of the platoon. The entire platoon would be punished and we would receive additional woes.

Of course, we had no way of preventing fouls, or assisting recruits to learn skills – we weren't allowed to talk to each other for the first eight weeks. Our only recourse and unfortunate teaching method became "The Guide and Squad Leaders Counsel." After lights out, while lying in his bunk asleep, the turd of the day would be awakened, reminded of his infraction, advised to never repeat it, or screw up in any way, and then, with a pillow over the offender's face, he'd be beaten soundly about the chest, abdomen and back (no visible bruises) by all five of us. I'm not proud of it, but that's what happened.

Once, the platoon marched below expectations and we were all punished with a million push-ups, sit-ups, jumping jacks, and squat thrusts. After the mass torment, Senior Drill Instructor Staff Sergeant "Surly" called the guide and squad leaders forward. We raced to him and locked into attention.

"Platoon! Eyeballs! Did you maggots totally f*@# up today?"

"Sir, yes, sir!" shouted 68 adolescents.

"Well, do ya think that P.T. for the last two hours was enough punishment?"

"Sir, no, sir!" louder than the last reply.

"You pussies are one–hundred percent correct! And guess who's gonna pay – and pay dearly?"

"Sir, the privates, sir!"

"That's right! Startin' with these five. In the gear locker, you pukes! Now!"

We filed into the gear locker, a room 15 feet long by 10 feet wide and with nowhere to hide. We stood at attention shoulder to shoulder in a semi-circle. The D.I. fumed, breathed heavily, considered his attack. He turned the lights off, total darkness. I awaited certain death. A half minute went by in silence. The light blinked on.

"You are the luckiest sonsabitches on earth. I was afraid I'd kill ya, so I turned the light back on." He rolled up his sleeves, balled up his right fist and delivered a Mike Tyson blow to each of us on the jaw, promising death if we moved. He knocked me down. I flew over against some boxes, but picked myself up instantly and returned to my spot. He was infuriated, one of his recruits had fallen. He hit me again, on the other side of my jaw with his dominate hand. I fell again, figured my jaw was broken, but jumped back into place a quick as I could. He continued around the semi-circle unconcerned with me now.

After the beating, we were ordered to do squat thrusts, "until a thousand tiny sweat drops are in a puddle on the deck." (Squat thrusts are also called "burpies.") We exercised for 45 minutes before "Surly" got tired and ended our suffering.

We got more exercise after lights out. The Guide and Squad Leaders Counsel visited those responsible for our torture. I doubt that even today they've forgotten that evil day at Parris Island.

On a lighter note, one time McCoy rearranged assignments so that he and I stood fire watch together at the boathouse. For two hours in the middle of the night we were supposed to march around the secluded site. Instead, we made a lap now and again – in case someone was watching – and otherwise sat in the grass drinking sodas, eating chips and candy purchased from machines on site. Somehow McCoy knew about the machines and collected ten dollars in coins. We'd not had candy, chips, or sodas for ten weeks. It was heavenly.

I'll stop in a minute, but I'll tell ya this one, too. I became First Squad Leader because Pvt. Payne was fired from that position. He was a tall, lanky African-American, exactly the kind of kid the D.I.s like up front. I don't recall why he and the meanest man that's ever punched me, Sgt. Grimsley, started fighting, but it was spectacular. Both men were of the same build and complexion, Grimsley maybe five years older, and both knew how to throw some mean knuckle sandwiches.

They went round and round, Grimsley once spinning Payne like a top. He fell, and the Sgt. pounced and pounded the kid's face. The end came when both were exhausted and the D.I. pinned both of Payne's arms behind his back. He may have cried "uncle." Anyway, from that day forward Payne suffered unduly. The senior D.I. choked him out with his belt twice while demonstrating how to garrote the enemy. A different day, he slapped both of Payne's ears at the same time causing them to bleed, probably rupturing his ear drums. Payne had requested to pee, was denied, smacked, and told to piss his pants. He did. It became a cruel sport for the D.I.

Another good lesson for the rest of us was what happened to Barker. He was a big, corn-fed country boy unwilling to endure the programmed harassment and unable to keep his mouth shut. During an inspection one day after rifle range training, the D.I.s discovered 50 M-16 rounds (bullets) in Barker's foot locker. The sergeants made sure the whole platoon were witnesses. They called Barker to the front, interrogated him, slapped him around, and had him arrested. He went to jail – CCP, correctional custody platoon, where prisoners swam the motivation ditch three times each day of their sentence, remained covered in the slime and mud until their every third day shower, were served only bread and water, and ran everywhere they went. I saw him a couple of weeks later. The CCP prisoners were running to their next torture, Barker was handcuffed, arms behind his back. He was running backwards while the D.I. yanked the cuffs violently forcing Barker to keep pace.

While I was on Parris Island, one guy slit his wrists, one guy jumped off the third story, only breaking his legs, and one kid was thrown off the third story. I never found out by whom, probably some irritable visiting nun.

I stood opposite Pvt. "Puddinhead" in dental and watched three D.I.s surround him, one in each ear, the other nose to nose. The kid was already a wreck, weak and ill-suited for anything physically challenging or mentally stressful. They screamed at him, barked obscenities, cursed his bloodline, and promised horrid abuses. They were on him for three days, and I saw much of it. In the end he broke. He couldn't stand up straight, couldn't stop shaking, couldn't make a sound because he'd ruined his vocal cords screaming, "Yes, sir" and "No, sir."

The D.I. laughed as he told us about destroying "Puddinhead" and sending him home to mamma. I felt sorry for the kid and envisioned his proud mother collecting her broken boy from the bus station only a few weeks after she'd sent him away to become a man.

Let's tell a funny one – there are so few.

One evening we were all on line standing at modified attention with our hands held out, fingernails up to be inspected. Sgt. Medrono, the only sane D.I. on the island, walked up and down the rows of underwear-clad young men. He examined our ear hairs, our shaved faces, our finger and toe nails, our underwear, and made certain our names were stamped correctly on the clothing. He was a man of humor and made funny comments now and again, but by the rules, we weren't supposed to laugh. He came to Pvt. "Porky" and declared his ear hairs too long, his fingernails misshaped according to regulations, and his breath smelled like shit.

"Furthermore, Private Porkbelly, your shirt is the wrong size, it's too go**@mn tight! You can't breathe in that shirt and run from the gooks. They'll catchya in a heartbeat and eat your bacon butt with buzzard eggs for breakfast."

We tried to choke down our snickers. Medrono smacked Porky's hands down.

"You're too damn fat, Private Porky. What we gonna do with you? You're a slob and I will not have slobs in my Marine Corps. Your shirt's too small and your skivvies… Oh, my god, Private Porky! You got your skivvies (white cotton boxer shorts) on backwards!"

"Eyeballs! Look at this men. Private Porky's got his skivvies on backwards! Now ain't that convenient for your bunky!" he said and started to circle the private. "The pecker hole is in the back. Easy access! You bangin' your bunky, Private Porky?"

Medrono stood behind Porky and looked closely at the shorts. He erupted, "Oh, my god, Private Porky! You've got to be shittin' me! Where'd you get them skivvies, private?" He snatched Porky into the center of the aisle and twirled him around so we could all see.

"I can't believe it, Porky! This is absolutely un–f*#@in'–believable! You got on MY skivvies!"

Sure enough in crisp black ink "MEDRONO" was stamped on the underwear. They belonged to the Sergeant. I wanted to fall on the floor laughing. Medrono was hysterical. Porky changed on the spot, handed the boxers to Medrono who slammed them into the trash can, cursing and spewing.

Of course, I've got a bunch more, but they'll have to wait till I write my best seller, *Marine Corps Days.* Meanwhile, here's one for the road.

My favorite memory of boot camp is from the second to last day. Michael Hill's dad drove to P.I. two days before graduation, went through the proper channels, and checked us out like library books. We were summoned by our drill instructor, who detested the idea. He ordered us to wear our best green combat utilities and raincoat, gave instructions of where to go, when to return, and detailed the punishment we would receive when we got back. We dressed and exited as swiftly as possible. We were ordered to exit through our shower rooms, then the next platoons shower rooms, and finally across their quarterdeck. Somehow, I was elected to do the talking.

When we came to the other platoon's entryway, we locked our 18-year old bodies into attention. I slammed my right palm hard against the tiled wall, striking it within a red stenciled hand print and recited the approved solicitation.

Whack, whack, whack. Then as loud as possible, "Sir, Private Landolfi requests permission to speak to the drill instructor, or senior drill instructor, sir." No answer, I had to repeat this twice.

Finally, "Whaddaya want, worm?"

"Sir, the private requests permission to cross the drill instructor's, or senior drill instructor's quarterdeck, sir."

A long moment of silence.

"Com'mere, worm."

I quick-stepped into the foreign squad bay, my partners remained behind, hidden, safe. I snapped to a rigid, post-like attention directly in front of the D.I. He hated me. He wanted to kill me. He bent forward. His nose touched mine. Cheap black coffee and stale unfiltered cigarette breath. I was terrified.

"Eyeballs!" he called to his platoon. Sixty men were at attention, facing each other, standing on parallel black lines painted on the barracks floor. They twisted their heads around and locked their sights on me. The D.I. unfolded his torso and regained his enormous natural height. He'd been demonstrating how to spit-shine boots using a tee shirt, polish, and lighter fluid.

"You got some kinda nerve, you little puke, asking to cross my quarterdeck."

He shined the boot for another second, then dropped it and the cloth. I stood absolutely still, petrified, eyes locked onto a point in space beyond the giant. He strutted slowly around me, upended the lighter fluid can and squirted the volatile liquid on the floor in a circle around me. Round and round he went until the can was empty.

Nose to nose again, rancid breath, "Know what I'm gonna do, worm?"

At full volume, "Sir, yes, sir! Burn the private up, sir!"

"Ya gottam right." He stepped back, struck a match and let it fall.

Flames engulfed me. I hesitated, remained at attention for a second then, stepped out of the circle of fire. He went berserk, hopped up and down, ordered me back into the flames, cursed me with every venomous word he knew and whipped his arms around so violently I was certain he'd knock me unconscious. In three seconds, I stepped back into the circle, taking my chances with third degree burns instead of the maniac. His rant continued, but I stepped back out and held my ground this time, the plastic raincoat exploding into flames worrying me more than he did.

He couldn't believe it. I stood outside "his ring of fire." His face turned red, nose flattened mine, spit flew as he cursed me, my mother and my future children. His fists were wrecking balls, his arms drew back – cocked to kill, the veins in his neck ready to explode. He pulled in two huge breaths, stood up straight, removed the .45 from its holster, pressed the barrel into my forehead right between my eyes. Another loud breath.

"Permission granted. Run, you little shit. Run for your life!"

I did and my buddies almost ran me over.

We enjoyed two hours of nearly forgotten freedoms: speaking at will, sitting on padded seats, menu choices and restaurant food, ice cream and candy, riding in a Cadillac.

We didn't have to cross the maniac's squad bay to return to our barracks. We went in our front door. I've always wondered why we didn't leave through that same door. Was it all part of some evil plan?

Let's end on a more positive note: a final 5-minute story.

The Good Things

I was pedaling up a steep mountain trail, breathing hard, heart pounding, and sweat dripping off my nose. It was rather brutal, but good exercise that helps keep me young. As I neared the top, I considered how hard the climb had been, how hard everything had been recently. It had been a difficult year, with lots of family drama.

Recollections flashed through my mind and I lost focus for a moment. Suddenly, I was on top and headed down. Painful memories faded as I shifted gears, turned the pedals and coasted downhill.

The trail was smooth; the air was cool. I couldn't help but smile. A thought pried its way into my consciousness. Think of all the good things. Focus on all the wonderful things that have happened.

I'd pedaled that trail a thousand times so, I let my mind wonder.

I remembered my first kiss with Kelly. She wrapped me in loving arms and held me tight. Our eyes locked and my heart jumped. I was breathless. I saw her excitement, her passion for me. Yes, me. Without words our lips drew near and met. Electricity. Fireworks. Heat. Chills. My heart beat wildly, almost burst. The moment lasted an eternity and ended too soon. God, that was wonderful. Let's do it again.

My mind jumped around, thought of commonalities, positive moments we could all appreciate.

What about the first time your parent let go and you pedaled away, all on your own, maybe a little wobbly, but you held your balance. You could ride a bike, all by yourself. You couldn't stop grinning; the smile hurt your face. The wind in your hair was evidence of new freedom. You could join the other kids, you were growing up, jumping life's hurdles. Making mom proud.

The most precious were the times when you were young, maybe too young to remember with mental images, but certainly with warm, peaceful feelings of unconditional, undying love and trust. You were a small child and mom held you close. She rocked you and sang with a beautiful voice her hopes for you, her love for you. You were her dream come true. You completed her. You two were a team, inseparable and unconquerable. Pure love.

That's pretty mushy, but it's all true and positive.

What about that crazy kitten chasing the autumn leaf skittering down the driveway in the breeze. Fluffy went pouncing and batting, springing up as though yanked by invisible puppet strings, the dried-up leaf skidding back and forth evading capture, taunting the apoplectic pet. That put a smile on everyone's face.

Life is so full of wonderful moments. Why is it so easy to focus on the negative aspects, the painful, the irritations?

I zipped down the trail and hit a jump, not an X-Games stunt, but I got some air and landed like an expert. Where were the cameras? Man, that was fun. The light bulb flashed. This is the best moment of your life, the only moment you have. Be in the moment, relish it, pull it in and live it fully. There really is nothing else. Now is all you have. It's not a memory that may slip, become irretrievable. It's not a hope for the future that may never occur. Now cannot be stolen; it's all yours, so make it the finest moment of your life.

I skidded to a stop overlooking a clear running stream and the mountain's slope. I caught my breath and contemplated the Zen of Now. And Joy. And Positive Thinking.

Steer your thoughts away from anything negative; focus on the innumerable beautiful miracles of life. Close your eyes and see them, be them:

The loving wave of your children as you drive off to work.

The shade of a tree on a hot summer day.

Ice water after mowing the lawn.

Sleeping late on Saturday morning.

Holding your lover during a snowstorm.

A warm shower after a long journey.

Comfortable shoes.

I sat in the leaves, transfixed on the sight and sounds of the stream and surrounding forest, a miracle of creation, a healing elixir for my soul. My muscles relaxed, my frown lines faded. I conjured images of my father and brother, both now gone and reminded the forest of how they had loved it.

"Never forget," I spoke to my surroundings, "how my father loved to pedal your trails, counting the miles and the stream crossings. He memorized your features, gave names to your rocks and the hidden places high on your mountain flanks beneath rhododendron thickets. And never forget my brother's love for mountain peaks and secret streams with swimming holes and rope swings. Remember all the love we shared under your canopies of green oak and poplar leaves, or gnarly, bare winter branches."

The forest answered with a light puff of honeysuckle breeze and the voice of a raven soaring overhead. An incredible omen. A miraculous positive sign.

I pedaled off with only love in my heart and the positive energy of creation in my soul, in the "now," living the finest moment of my life and wishing to share the feeling with all of mankind.

The glass is not half full; it's overflowing.

Afterward

Well, there you have it. I hope you had as much fun reading as I did writing. I hope that somewhere in the many paragraphs you found a reason to smile, maybe even laugh. I hope your heart pounded and tears welled on occasion. I hope your gut twisted with uncomfortable subjects, or descriptions of macabre scenes. I hope my words painted vivid pictures that you'll recall while recommending this book to your neighbor. I hope that any troublesome tissues have benefited from new time management skills and my words have afforded you a little diversion from your hectic, stressful life.

Once again, I thank you for buying my book and for allowing me to become part of your life. I hope to write another one and tell you another story.

Michael Landolfi

CPSIA information can be obtained
at www.ICGtesting.com
Printed in the USA
LVHW09s1020130818
586812LV00001B/37/P

9 781506 138923